ON WRITING

(AND READING!)

SHORT

A Science Fiction Writer's Quest
for Stories That Matter

SKYFOX
PUBLISHING

RON COLLINS

On Writing (And Reading) Short
A Science Fiction Writer's Quest for Stories That Matter

Skyfox Publishing

Paperback ISBN-10: 1-946176-32-5
Hardcover ISBN-10: 1-946176-60-5

Paperback ISBN-13: 987-1-946176-32-X
Hardcover ISBN-13: 978-1-946176-60-8

Contents

Acknowledgments

I would like to thank my daughter, Brigid—who is a brilliant writer (already better than her dad), and a fantastic collaborator, both as a writer and an editor. If you love middle grade/YA work in a speculative fiction setting, you owe it to yourself to get hold of her Sugimori Sisters collections. I consider them to exist in the space between Ray Bradbury and Calvin and Hobbes, updated. Her fantasy and fey world work is brilliant, too. In the case of *On Writing (and Reading) Short*, though, I want to also thank her for being a helpful guinea pig as a first reader.

I want to thank all the people who make up my own version of Write Club. There are literally hundreds. So, um, you know who you are.

And, of course, I need to thank my wife, Lisa, for once again applying her deft work as my copy editor (insert classic "all errors mine" here), and I want to thank her for … well … pretty much everything else that is good.

Kickstarter Backers

Finally, I want to give a special spotlight to the Kickstarter project that launched the publication of this book, and of course the may backers who made this project happen. Thank you so much for helping my celebration of short fiction so, um, jovial! So many thanks to:

A. J. Payler A.M. Roark Alison Naomi Holt Andy F Anna McCluskey Annie Reed Anonymous (aggregated) Anthea Sharp Bence Mitlasóczki Beth Paul Bethany Tomerlin Prince Britt Malka Bugz Caleb Monroe Carolyn Rowland Céline Malgen Charley Marsh Christopher R Corrie Garrett CW Hawes D. Crowe Dale Ivan Smith Danielle Williams David H Hendrickson Dean Wesley Smith Diana Deverell Emily L Erin Eron Wyngarde Eva Holmquist Fabien Delorme Felicia Fredlund Fellow Writer Filip Magnus Fiona L. Woods Frank Theodat Gage "SpaceGhoat" Troy Holly Pickett Hope Terrell Ifeanyi Esimai Irette Y Patterson Isaac R Howard Jacen Leonard Jack Schiller Jackie Heelein James Husum James Palmer Jerry Ackerman Jim Gotaas Joe Cron Johanna Rothman Joseph & Jules Procopio Justin Alexander Dorsey Kalvin Chinyere, M.D. Karen Fonville Kari & Jason Kat Feels Kathryn Kaleigh Keith West, Future Potentate of the Solar System Kelly Washington Kelvin Neely Ken Talley Kevin Dickson Kim Brooks Laura Ware Lawrence Dunmore Len C Leslie Claire Walker Li Leung Wang Linda Niehoff Lisa Owen Lisa Silverthorne Liz Lazo Luke EisBrenner M. L. Buchman Mark Posey Mary Jo Rabe Mervi Hamalainen Michael A. Burstein Michael Barbato-Dunn Michael Feir Michael McComas Michael Warren Lucas Michelle Kitz Niz Thomas Pablo Cárdenas Oliveros Peggy Kurilla Pierino Gattei Quintin R.S. Kellogg Randy A McCallum Rebecca

Buchanan Rich Steeves Richard Schneck Rob Cornell Rob Vagle
Robert B Battle Robert K Barbour Ronald H. Miller Ryan M.
Williams Saleh G Samuel Barton Sara McAninch Sarah Ettritch
Sharon Bass – Super Beta! Sharon Markatcheff Stefon Mears
Stephannie Tallent Stephen and Carolyn Ivy Stein T. Thorn Coyle
Thorsten Daniel Vera Nazarian Zoe Cannon

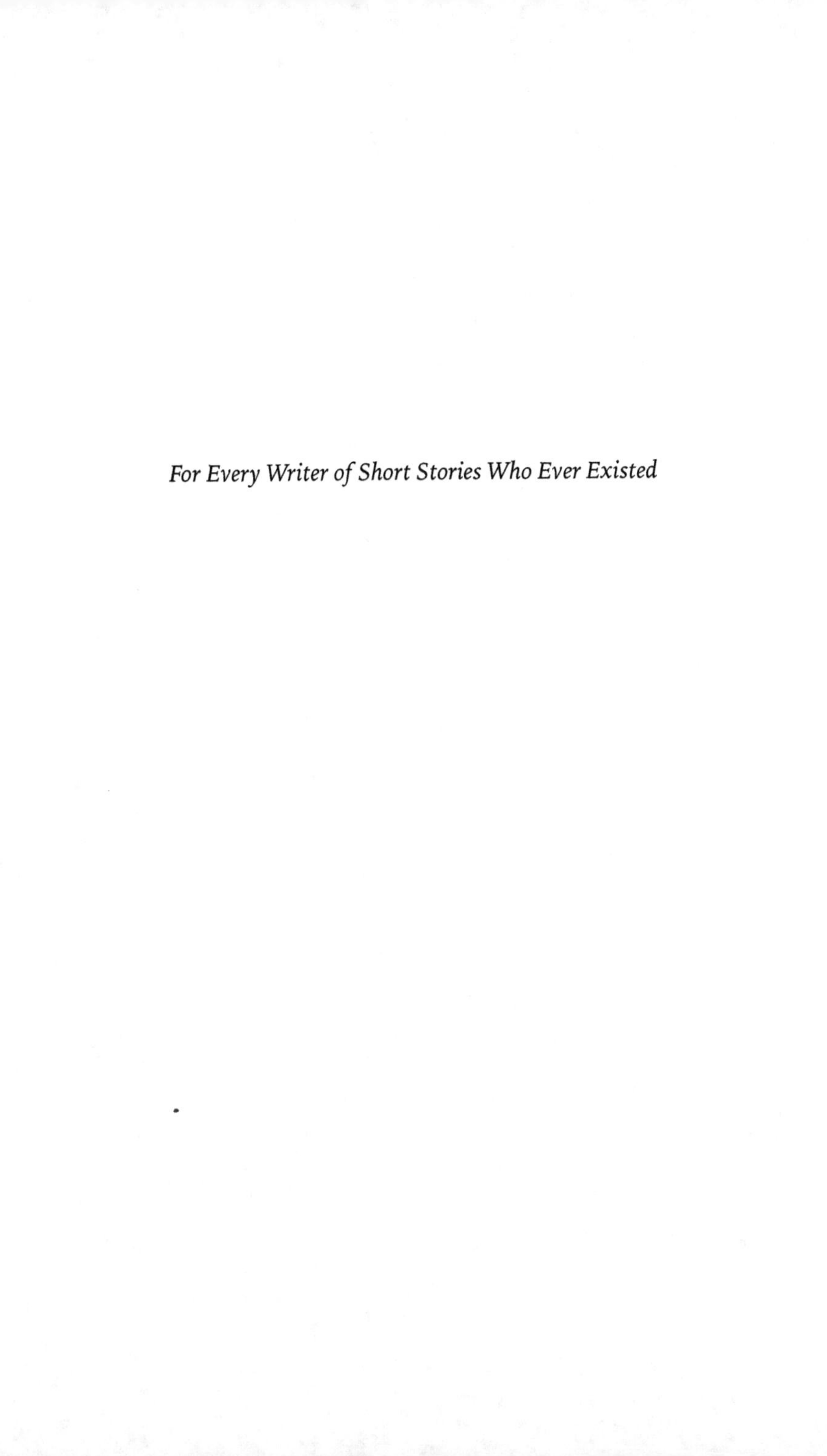

For Every Writer of Short Stories Who Ever Existed

Introduction

This book has its roots in a series of posts I made to my blog that I titled "Adventures of a First-Time Editor," and that expounded on the events surrounding the creation of *Face the Strange*, an anthology that I co-edited with my daughter, Brigid. That project was great fun, and the result was an amazing book.

Those posts were fun to write, too, and also made me realize I had something to say about writing and about short stories in particular. So you can blame the existence of this book on that anthology and on the workshop it sprang from.

It's been an illuminating book to write.

This is because I'm the kind of writer who often comes to the page to figure out how I feel or how I think about something that's happened, and this book is the first time in a while that I've spent any real time thinking about what I do or why I do it. All I knew in starting it was that I wanted to focus mostly on short fiction. Sure, I knew it would have to slide into the territory of "all writing" often enough, but I've spent a lot of my life enjoying short works. I wanted to stay there as long as I could.

I wanted to come at this from the point of view of a reader as well as that of a writer, too, because that's how we all come to this writing gig, right?

We write because we read. It's the reader inside that drives us, and I do so love short stories.

If you do, too, maybe parts of this book will stoke that passion.

Maybe, in the middle of a passage, I'll say something that will make your fingers itch with desire so strong as to make you want to pick up a piece you really love, and read it all over again. Or maybe it will make you go to an issue of your favorite publication or your favorite author's website and introduce yourself to something new from them.

That would make me happy.

Because, sure, I'm going to talk about writing in this book—sometimes in pretty deep ways—but in the end, everything revolves around reading.

Ron Collins
Oro Valley
2022

Why Short Stories?

IF I WERE the Grand Emperor of the Universe, short story writers would never have to pay for a dinner. Ever. Their bank accounts would overflow, they would always go to the front of any line that exists, and the sun would shine from behind them every time they made an entrance.

There is a feeling in a short story that cannot be found in a novel—a sense of being on a tightrope, this feeling that a writer has opened a vein into their soul and squeezed out just that most potent dram of the distilled essence of self that takes a reader's breath away.

I know.

That sounds so dramatic, doesn't it?

How are we supposed to believe you, Ron, when you hit us with that kind of woo-woo?

It's true, though.

A good short story can change my day. A great one can change my life.

I fully accept that this makes me weird.

My whole life is like that, I suppose. I'm the kind of person who, if given a chunk of dark chocolate, will immediately chomp it up so the cocoa blast hits my senses full speed, then explodes into chocolate smithereens. My wife, who is more levelheaded, will leave that same chocolate block to dissolve on her tongue for as long as it will last. I can already feel her eyes rolling at me for presenting my obviously superior method as so obviously superior, but that too is life.

Did I mention my wife is the kind of person who can take or leave a short story?

Sad. I know.

Luckily, the short story is not a jealous love.

It does not require exclusivity. And, since I try to be one of those "and" people rather than an "or" person (gimme both *Star Trek* and *Star Wars,* all right?), I am free to admire a great novella or novel just as well as a brilliant short story.

Or comic.

Or movie. Or…

Just say yes.

Life is too short to be grumpy all day.

But there's something special about a short story.

Something that feels important.

Sometimes it seems like the short story is the runt of the litter, the everyperson, the weary huddled masses yearning to be free. No one cares about the short story. It is the discarded one, the overlooked or ignored child, the one—for some reason that escapes me—seen as of lesser value. Perhaps this feeling that short stories are the lesser of literature's siblings is because they are often—but embarrassingly not always—quicker to write. Perhaps readers think they can feel the writer bleeding over a novel but can dismiss short stories as simply things dashed out on a series of larks.

Who can tell?

All I can say for sure is that it's annoying, that for my "burst of chocolate" taste, the short story is *often* far more interesting than a novel.

Not "better," and not "always," but "more interesting" and "often."

I am a reader who cannot let short stories go.

Unlike their ponderous siblings in the novel, a short story is generous with its time. It makes its point in bursts of story-laced enjoyment, then steps aside to leave me stewing on it. The short story is a place where writers can take massive risks, too, so they can feel more edgy and daring.

Try, for example, to write a story that reads sentence-by-sentence in perfect reverse order, as Daniel Quinn did in his oddly marvelous tale "The Frog King, or Iron Henry," published in the anthology *Black Thorn, White Rose*. Try to write Mike Resnick's "Winter Solstice," a story that twists the Merlin legend. Or Rachel Swirsky's "If You Were a Dinosaur, My Love."

Or my own "After" (which I will include here simply because I can), which is a story told in a single (albeit long) sentence.

These things can be done in short stories, and once I see them I am somehow changed.

These pieces are delicate. Difficult pieces.

They would fall apart as novels.

So, yes, there's something beautiful in a short story.

Something dashing and magical about them.

Something pristine.

AFTER

IT'S ONLY after you train all your life (giving up weekends and ballgames and late nights at the club to study control systems and thermodynamics, then later checklists of launch processes, the physics of re-entry, and the thousands of other things they stuff into your head), after you find it's a simple mechanical failure that causes all the trouble, an Allen wrench in basic black which was not designed to fall into the airlock mechanism but most certainly does fall into that same mechanism, only after you find yourself on the wrong side of the ship's skin, watching as Dag and Trina and Lane go bat-shit crazy trying all the things from all the manuals, guides, and computer simulations that they gave up their nights and ballgames and weekends to study (and then try a few hundred more things that aren't in those manuals), after you realize they can't think of anything else and you're still out here and you cut yourself loose to spare their feelings and you rotate slowly into space for hours, or days, or weeks while your suit drains its battery pack and you shut off the heads-up to save the last few minutes, only after all that work, and pain, and suffering, that you look with your oxygen-starved brain into a universe so deep with its stars and galaxies, with its novae and pulsars and other things you cannot even pretend to imagine, that you say to yourself, "My God, how beautiful you are.

First Memories

Even when I was a kid, I envisioned myself as a writer.

My first story, written when I was probably nine or ten, was a marvelous piece of work titled "The Great Train Robbery." It was a short story, of course, but I "published" it as a limited edition novel—with a one-copy run—including creating a great cover done up in blue marker and bound with ties of yarn or string, and complete with a series of blurbs that celebrated me as the "Great Writer" that I was.

I remember having fun.

I read short stories in school simply because they were assigned.

You know the ones: Hawthorne and Poe, et cetera. I remember not being particularly thrilled by them, but I think that's mostly because they were required reading rather than self-motivated adventuring. Cliché or not, I was obstinate—not particularly open of the mind.

You could make me do something, but you could not make me enjoy it.

I don't think I've ever been much of a Hawthorne fan—and it took me awhile to warm to Poe's particular brand of fiction.

Go figure, right.

I got my revenge by reading other things, though—short stories most definitely included.

Robert Louis Stevenson's *The Suicide Club and Other Stories* is affixed to my brain, for example. I can still see its cover with its dagger and its aces. I still recall the title story's dark intrigue.

A Google search just now brought me a warm smile of memory-ific satisfaction.

As I grew older, as one does, I lost touch with the short story.

I played basketball in high school…or rather I protected the bench from drifting away if gravity were to ever become reversed in the middle of the game.

I played guitar with my brother for a bit, though I only excelled at the opening bars of any song before growing bored with them. Let's just say that if there is ever a market for opening riffs, I'm going to be rich. There was another problem with being a musician, though. Despite one side of my brain enjoying the attention of being on a stage, the other side found it all some-what boring, sometimes uncomfortable, and even a bit wearying. I wasn't really sure what I was doing, but I was more than a little certain I wasn't that good at it.

So, no, music wasn't for me.

While my brother went to L.A. to pursue becoming a rock star, I went to school, eventually becoming good enough at pretending to study calculus and FORTRAN that they called me —like my father before me—an engineer.

Yet still I'd write.

And when I wrote, it was always in the form of a short story.

One of my favorite memories is sitting poolside at a Holiday Inn and writing a short story from the point of view of a leopard lying in wait around an African water hole. I can still remember sitting there—blue ballpoint pen in hand (yes, I am old). The humid air was filled with the smell of chlorine, and an occasional crash or clatter of the world outside would impinge on my own world as the story flowed.

I knew even then that I liked short stories quite a lot.

They were different from novels.

Though I had given up thoughts of becoming a writer myself, I felt the existence of these stories as something important.

I was kind of a dunce back then, though.

I thought short stories came in two types: classic literature, and science fiction.

I don't mean that in the classic sense of dismissal of Science

Fiction. What I mean is that I was literally so oblivious to what was going on around me that I had no idea short stories existed outside the genres of classic literature and science fiction.

Yeah, I don't know what I was thinking, either.

Then I found Robert Lynn Asprin's *Thieves' World* anthologies, and the world came to a halt.

What?

Seriously?

It comes in pints?

As soon as I found that series, I read them all and I'd wait impatiently at the bookstore for the next to come out.

Sure, I read novels of all types and all genres, too—Stephen King, Orson Scott Card, Anne Rice, Dean Koontz, Truman Capote. Hemingway and Fitzgerald, Clancy and Fleming. Even Sidney Sheldon—a friend of mine at the time said she liked *The Other Side of Midnight* because she liked "earthy books" and I knew what that meant. Big books, small books, fantasy books, suspense and mystery. I loved Agatha Christy as much as the next guy.

But short stories were something different.

Even then I think I was trying to get my mind around how and why.

What Comes First?

Sometime back I got into a friendly if brief Internet spat with my good friend Myke Cole, an ex-Coast Guard officer and history fanatic who has written several fine novels. It started when he said you cannot learn to write a novel by writing short stories.

His viewpoint is not really out of the norm. I think a lot of mistaken people feel that way.

As you can tell from my phrasing, I am not one of those people.

I think all forms of writing can, in general, be used to help learn all other forms. That said, Myke and his acolytes are not completely wrong. The novel is certainly a different beast than the short story. So, it's certainly *possible* that a novel requires a different skillset to write than a short story does. In fact, I agree that much, at least, is probably true.

The problem, however, is that Myke has the polarity reversed.

You most certainly *can* learn to write novels by writing short stories.

This has always been true and will always be true. Simply the fact that, when I was a baby writer, the primary path into the publishing industry was through the short markets proves this beyond any real argument.

So, the idea you cannot learn to write novels by writing short stories is demonstrably false.

I think, however, the counter—that you cannot learn to write short fiction by writing novels—may well be right.

How could we find out?

Hmm.

Well, at the risk of feeling like I'm going back to elementary school, I think I'll try to determine it this way.

Let's start by asking ourselves, just what is a short story?

What Is a Short Story?

JOHN HELFERS—AN editor friend of mine—has a phrase he uses sometimes when asked how to write a short story: "Two characters, one problem, and 3,000 words," he will say.

As a broad idea, that's pretty good.

A writer can go a long way simply by taking that framework to heart, anyway. When I look at my own work, I see John's maxim applies often enough.

There are exceptions, because of course there are.

The love triangle comes to mind (three characters), or the buddy story in which two protagonists struggle against a single antagonist (with, again, three characters). If you spend five minutes thinking about it, you'll find lots of exceptions. The word *character* in that definition can be stretched too, especially for us writers of speculative fiction. "Man versus nature," for instance, can become "mouse versus magic." Or, "Person vs. Society," in which the group can be a character.

So, grumble.

John's definition has other flaws, too: Short stories can certainly have more than one fundamental problem to resolve, and in most cases will wind up over 3,000 words. The Science Fiction Writers of America defines a short story as anything under 7,500 words, other groups have other definitions.

If you want to see exactly how complex a short story can be in a very few words, you could do worse than to read the lyrics to Bob Dylan's "Lily, Rosemary and the Jack of Hearts," in which Dylan uses something less than 900 words to introduce us to four primary characters, each with briefly sketched but well-defined backgrounds, and each with their own set of problems.

The story is full of intrigue and deceit, too, with at least four distinct plot lines going on. There's a bank robbery, and lost loves all around. The hazy influence of the law sits at a table getting drunk until it's called on to administer something we'll agree to call justice in the end. The song carries a commentary on capitalism and roguishness. It explores the role of power and freedom in relationships. Its outcome is dramatic and hinges on vengeance. When one dwells on the situations within, we see the influence of gender roles maintained by each character.

Its validation is perfect.

Every stanza could be expanded into its own chapter, and the entire work could then make a riveting novel. But Dylan distills it all into 900 words, and still manages to resolve everything in ways that are deeply satisfying.

I suppose there's a reason he's a Nobel Prize winner.

Still, John's point of view is useful, not because it specifically defines a short story, but because it helps put boundaries in place that the writer can use to hit their target.

Still, this is annoying.

I'm out here looking for a definition, and boundaries are not definitions.

Without said definition, how are we to determine what skills we need to write a novel versus a short story?

It really feels like we should be able to define this.

So, let's pull the old dictionary gambit.

The Oxford Languages Dictionary says a short story is one *with a fully developed theme but significantly shorter and less elaborate than a novel.*

Hmm.

That's not really helpful, either.

What is *significantly*, after all?

Fifty percent? Seventy-five? Or, how about twenty-five percent? I'm pretty sure a retailer giving me a 25% discount would consider that a significant price cut. Does that work for us? If a novel is 100,000 words, does that mean a short story can be 75,000?

I don't think so.

I think most folks would look at a 75,000 word manuscript and say "now there's a novel!"

And exactly how much less *elaborate* can we be?

Bob Dylan wants to know.

All right that last line was just me being prissy.

Let me be clear. I do not know Bob Dylan. I have no idea whether he wants to know exactly how elaborate he can be while writing a short story and still have it qualify as such. It's likely he does not much care.

In that light, I figure we might all be able to learn something from Dylan's frame of mind, but I digress.

NOT HAPPY WITH the Oxford dictionary definition, I turned to the next best thing: the Wisdom of the Crowds that is Wikipedia, which today includes this definition: *A short story is a piece of prose fiction that typically can be read in one sitting and focuses on a self-contained incident or series of linked incidents, with the intent of evoking a single effect or mood.*

Again, hmmm.

This is getting frustrating.

Other than length (defined here as one sitting), how is that any different from a novel?

And really, who among us has not finished off a novel in one sitting?

Finally, there's this from the Blurb website: *A short story is a work of prose fiction that can be read in one sitting—usually between 20 minutes to an hour. There is no maximum length, but the average short story is 1,000 to 7,500 words, with some outliers reaching 10,000 or 15,000 words. At around 10 to 25 pages, that makes short stories much shorter than novels, with only a few approaching novella length. A piece of fiction shorter than 1,000 words is considered a "short short story" or "flash fiction," and anything less than 300 words is rightfully called "microfiction."*

So, there we have it.

All the experts.

For my taste they all seem to be dancing around the subject.

Either way, though, when I read either a short story or a novel, I want to walk away satisfied. And that requires a writer to be able to tell a story. As far as I can tell then, the definition of a short story is simply a story that has fewer words than a novel. After this quest I am now forced to conclude that, yes, this seems to be what a short story is. That both novels and short stories are —regardless of size—stories…

…and that a short story is a story that is short.

How short?

Well, um, short.

And that a novel is a story that is long.

How long?

Hmmm.

Let's not do that again, shall we?

Perhaps we could view a novel, then, as a gathering of short stories (or novelettes, or novellas)—each twining through a longer (or larger) narrative, and each with their own characters, and problems, and strivings to win.

Having written both novels and short stories, I admit I like this basic idea.

If you like it too, then you'll see why I suggest that a writer needs to know how to write an effective short story if they are going to write a successful novel.

Sneaky, right?

Take that, you Cole acolytes!

A Take on Interesting

It's true. Reading a novel *feels* different from reading a short story.

Novels can wander. Novels can explore. That's their beauty, of course. A good novel takes the reader away from the moment and lets us live in another universe. Which, I think, is their purpose. A great novel lets me escape the world we live in for large chunks of time.

I have to commit to a novel, though. When I crack open the book, I am agreeing to spend time with it—agreeing to bring my own sensibilities forward to create a magical transfer of story from the author's mind to mine.

Until, of course, something goes wrong, anyway.

A detail there.

A characterization that falls flat or dialog that stilts.

Still, though, after I've committed myself as a reader, the novel writer might get some leeway. Might get a pass for a lazy phrase here or there. Might survive me skimming past a chunk of text I find less enthralling (can we say Tom Bombadil, you Tolkien lovers out there?).

How much can a writer get away with?

Well?

That's a good question.

The answer, I think, can be found in the word *interesting*.

This is something short stories and novels have in common: They have to be interesting.

All the time.

I've taken to saying that a writer can break any rule in the book as long as they are interesting. It is, in fact, fun to break rules that way. And the mere breaking of these rules can—of itself—be interesting. So, yeah, a writer can get away with a lot. But you can never be *not* interesting.

Here's an example.

Mike Resnick was one of my favorite short story writers of all time. This is not because he was a mentor of mine, but because he was really, really good. Good enough to be the most decorated speculative fiction writer of all time.

He began his award-winning short story "The 43 Antarean Dynasties," in this fashion.

To THANK *the Maker Of All Things for the birth of his first male offspring, the Emperor Maloth IV ordered his architects to build a temple that would forever dwarf all other buildings on the planet.*

THIS IS A THING OF BEAUTY.

Mike could have started with this line: *To thank God for the birth of his first son the emperor ordered his architects to build the biggest temple of all time.*

This generic sentence says essentially the same thing, and in fact it says it in fewer words—which is something short story writers covet. Yet it is nowhere near as precise and nowhere near as interesting. My example carries very little weight when compared to Mike's choices. His *Maker of All Things* speaks of a specifically different culture than my generic *God*. His use of the term *first male offspring* carries similar weight. Naming the emperor gives us a person rather than a character, and the choice of that specific name moves us away from our current historical timeline and suggests something different is coming.

When I read the phrase *"would forever dwarf all other buildings on the planet,"* I am cemented into the story.

Note something interesting here (he says without irony).

There is no sensory information in Mike's first sentence.

No sounds or tastes or smells. No colors. Nothing at all visual.

This breaks a rule now, doesn't it?

Readers want to be thrown directly into the story, and writers are taught to do that by making these first sentences tactile. But note something else—despite the lack of anything close to a tactile word appearing in it, as I read that first sentence I can taste dust and sense heat. Resnick's choices feel almost Egyptian to me, and despite the fact that his last word places me on an alien planet, I already have a feel for the place and its culture.

Resnick knew the rules, though. He proceeds over the next several sentences to draw me down deeper and deeper into this setting. Even then however he will be stingy with his descriptive elements, focusing my attention on legend and purpose rather than on place and time.

It is a marvelous example of how to be interesting.

As an aside, I learned at one point that Mike was at least some-what colorblind, and from that moment it made me wonder if he had learned to be so precise in other areas specifically as a result.

We use what we have, right?

THIS UNRELENTING NEED TO be interesting is the realm of the short story, though.

A short story writer has to get on with it, but must also create depth.

And since the reader of short stories does not need to commit as much effort as the reader of a novel, I pontificate that their leash is that much shorter. Every word is an off-ramp, after all. You can lose me at any point of the way. A short story, to be successful, has to be deeply interesting all the time in ways a novel does not. To truly succeed, a short story needs to be precise.

I'd say this is another reason you can more rapidly learn to write novels by writing short stories, and why you can write a novel but still need to learn something to write a short story.

I can enjoy a lazy novel at times, but I won't finish a lazy short story—unless, of course, it's about...um...baseball.

Baseball?

What the hell does that mean, right?

Well, let's just see...

Reader Cookies

Writing (and therefore reading) is a very personal business—not in the vein of "who you know," though there is some of that, but more in the fact that every person who makes any piece of art throws at least a piece of themselves into it, and that the perceived quality of that work is so, so subjective. And the way we talk about that quality leads to us being judgmental in ways we may not even realize

One person's ... trash ... is another's treasure.

Gardner Dozois, who edited *Asimov's Science Fiction* for many years, would talk about reader cookies—elements of a story that, when he came upon them, were like being passed a plate of oven-fresh cookies. When that happened, he would just eat them up.

I like that.

We all have these reader cookies. I know I do.

A baseball story, for example, will always catch my eye and once I'm into it—unless the author does something remarkably outrageous—you can pretty much assure I'll finish it no matter what. It's also a good bet that I'll be happy. Will Casey strike out? Will there be a great play to save the game? A hidden ball trick? I want to know.

I mean, I really want to know.

I have other reader cookies, too. We all do. But almost any baseball story will get me reading, and a good baseball story can get me literally bouncing on my seat.

Likewise, we all also have *anti-reader cookies*, things we just don't want to read about.

I am not, for example, much on zombies.

This actually makes me sad, or in truth a little embarrassed.

I like to think I'm openminded. I keep telling myself I

shouldn't be so discriminatory, that I'm sure there are several very good stories written around zombies. I've probably read a few and just don't remember them. *Come on, Ron,* I say to myself. *Lots of other people love them. Just give one a chance.*

Alas, while I can make myself read zombie fiction, I just cannot make myself become thrilled with the idea.

This does not make me a bad human, it makes me a human human.

As a writer it means that if the story I'm writing hits an editor's reader cookie or an anti-reader cookie, I'm going to get a reaction that may go beyond the "quality" of the story in either direction.

A rejection does not mean my story sucks (though it could, I suppose).

All it means is that the editor did not like it.

Of course, it's also possible the editor loved it, but maybe already had something like it in inventory, and didn't want to create cross-traffic. For example, if I am ever editing anthologies again, unless I'm editing an actual baseball-themed project I'll probably take only one baseball story. So, as a writer, there's a weird game theory aspect to deciding to write to an editor's known reader cookies. If everyone does it, no one wins.

To make matters worse, every editor—just like every reader—is different.

Editor #1 may reject an award-quality story simply because that editor hates baseball, and then Editor #2 passes because they already have one ready to come out.

Life, as they say, is a bitch.

But—as crazy as it is to hate baseball—in its own way I admit this aspect of the world's unfairness is what makes it beautiful.

Who wants to live in a world where everyone loves the same things?

Stories That Matter

LIKE A LOT OF PEOPLE, the first thing I wrote when I got "serious" about writing for publication was a short story. I was successful as far as that goes—the story was finished, and even eventually published. The fallout of that day, however, is even now somewhat embarrassing.

I was working as an engineer, and I'd been given an assignment that would eventually keep me in Washington D.C. for six weeks. I'd been put up in a "furnished apartment," which meant it had a kitchen full of plates, a broken-down couch, and a computer with a hard drive that did not ... drive. After doing touristy things my first Saturday, I asked myself what I was going to do with my time.

Write, I thought.

I'd always wanted to, after all. Suddenly I had time. And no one had to see it.

That last was kind of embarrassing, you know?

Having people see me, this kid engineer, thinking he might be able to write something worthwhile? That was crazy talk.

But here I was. Nobody watching.

Perfect.

I wrote a short story that night: My first since those exercises I'd done for college.

It was a lot of fun, so later that evening—filled with the effervescent energy that comes from only the act of creation—I rumbled down to the bookstore and picked up a thick tome titled *The Novel and Short Story Writer's Market*.

I was doing my homework, you see.

I had a family to support. Now an experienced hand, I needed to know if I could make money with this writing thing.

After paging through this big book, I was doubly certain this gig was for me.

I wanted to write science fiction, and this book laid out facts about the market for such tales. *Asimov's* published essentially twelve issues a year, and (say) eight stories a pop. That's 96 stories. And then there was *Analog* that worked at the same rate. And *Omni*. And *Weird Tales*, and all sorts more. The fields were lush, the game most definitely afoot.

I mean, seriously. Add up all that space and you get literally thousands of short stories being published every year.

How hard could it be?

THAT PEAL of rolling thunder you hear is the combined laughter of every writer on the planet.

I LICENSED my first story for publication in late 1994. I remember finding out I was going to be published by asking the editor, a man named Ewan Grantham, how to pronounce his first name. His response was: *"You pronounce it The Guy Who Just Bought Your First Story."*

As firsts go, that one's pretty fun.

I had started trying to write professionally in the very late eighties, so you can do the timeline math.

Along the way I read every writer's help books I could get my hands on. I was clearly focused on speculative fiction because—well, who wouldn't be? Speculative fiction is cool. It's fun. It's got a great beat and you can dance to it. But I read how-to books of every stripe.

At the time there was no real independent publishing—only traditional markets, both short and long.

This meant there was only one way into the industry: through the gatekeepers.

Playing the game according to Hoyle meant writing short stories—which were looked at as the minor leagues for bigger publishing houses. New writers broke into *Asimov's* or *F&SF* or *Analog*, or more likely several of them, and eventually an editor who you'd meet at a convention would politely ask if you had a novel.

Then the game was on.

So I spent a lot of time looking at markets and wondering what Agent X and Editor Y were looking for right now, or reading all the short work in *Asimov's, F&SF,* and *Analog* in hopes I could divine what Gardner Dozois, or Kris Rusch, or Stanley Schmidt was buying. I hung around chat rooms. I hobnobbed with editors at those conferences. In short, I did everything I could do to figure out how to get someone to take me in.

Everything that is, except the one thing that really mattered.

Even then I knew I could write.

But my work was spotty. This story would feel right, this other one not so much.

Looking back on it, I see now what I was missing.

I was working hard. Very hard. Working on my basic craft, and working on understanding the business as it existed at that time. What I wasn't doing was more important, though.

I would write anything, you see?

I wasn't purposefully focusing on things I cared about. In fact, I'm sure there were times I shied away from things simply because they were too close to the bone.

IN THE EARLY 2000s I hit a very dry spell.

I'd been publishing work for seven years, but I was tired, and my work wasn't where I wanted it to be. My day job was suddenly getting huge, and then there was the fact that this was right after 9/11, and that affected a lot of things in weird ways.

I slowed down at first.

Kind of retreated.

A step or two at a time, I let myself slip away from the keyboard. Let myself spend a week just batting manuscripts back into the void, or gave myself authorization to just go off to soak up the world, or hobbled along on with whatever crutch was handy at the time until I eventually realized I wasn't really creating words at all. One day I read an exercise my daughter, Brigid—that same Brigid who would later become an amazing writer and my *Face the Strange* co-editor—had done for school in which she said she'd seen me decide to quit writing. She wrote that she found a certain power in that act. If I could change my mind, she could, too.

I was happy she learned a lesson, and I do think that's a good lesson. But I asked myself at the time: Was that an actual decision?

Did I really decide to quit?

The answer was no.

So I returned.

As fates and Write Club would have it (he says in a bold move of foreshadowing), a short while later I was in a workshop talking to other writers.

As these things have a tendency to do, we were talking about business and, in particular, a writer's brand. Some knew their brands. Others didn't. I flashed on something Robert Sawyer said about how he viewed his own work, and suddenly realized I was just kind of floating around. Sometimes I would write something that made me feel good, and other times I was just trying to shoehorn work into a market.

I stewed about this on the trip home and, sitting on the airplane, I took a pen and on a piece of paper wrote "Stories That Matter."

I sat there, stunned, realizing that this was my brand.

Or, rather, this was the brand I wanted.

"Stories That Matter to who?" I thought to myself as I circled the phrase three times.

Then I smiled as I realized the answer was obvious.

Stories That Matter to Me.

The Only Truth

WHAT CAN I say about the craft of writing—short stories or not —that hasn't been said before?

Well, how about this: The best way to get better is to practice.

Hmmm…you've heard that, have you?

Okay.

Then let's try this: To be honest, you can stop after this next sentence.

Just write.

That's it. Nothing I say, or nothing any other writer who has written a how-to book can say, will do you much better than that.

Sure, you should read lots of books about the craft. If you love reading, and especially if you love writing, hearing writers talk about their world is always fascinating. Listening to writers can fill my heart, which then can make me itch to write. There's value to that.

I still read books on writing simply because they make me feel less alone, too.

Less strange, as it were.

There are lots of great books on how to think about craft, and you should certainly find them. But you need what you need, which will be different from what I need, so I don't think I can help you except to say you should find books that speak to you. For me those books were:

1. *Science Fiction Writer's Workshop-I: An Introduction to Fiction Mechanics* by Barry Longyear
2. *Writing to the Point: A Complete Guide to Selling Fiction* by Algis Budrys
3. *Bird by Bird* by Anne Lamott

This is because I needed to learn story structure, and I needed to come to grips with what it meant to bring myself emotionally to the page every day—that my fears and worries did not mean I was crazy.

If you need these things, perhaps these books will work for you.

I don't know.

But if you've made it here, just go write. Trust me. It's for the best.

Really, it is.

Lather, rinse, repeat.

The Second Only Truth

IF YOU'RE STILL READING after that last section, I'm going to try once more to save you some time.

While craft alone is enough to succeed, it is not enough to sustain.

So be yourself.

You are the only you on this planet. If you write, and if you write from your own place, you will eventually become the writer that only you can become. The best way to learn who that is will be by opening the lid to those things inside you and expose how you really think and feel, then write from within that.

I wish it were not true, but in my experience, the two most important things about creating anything are: (1) you have to just do it, and (2) only you can be you.

To Critique or Not to Critique, and How

IF YOU'RE A NEW WRITER, you're probably wondering if you should join a critique group.

We've all been there.

If you've ever thought about writing in any serious way, and especially if you've started later in life, it's almost certain you've run into the question of what to do with your work. How do I get better, you might ask. Or, more likely, am I secretly *already* the next Stephen King or James Patterson just waiting to be discovered?

Simply the thought of critique groups conjures up chilling images of intrepid young writers all with their metaphorical sleeves rolled up and blue pencils hovering, prepared to bleed over manuscripts so they can "help the author" make their story "better." The concept is akin to wind running sprints to get into shape. Barring track athletes, I figure no one else is really super-excited about running wind sprints, but everyone wants to get into shape.

** ASIDE: Give me a moment to be just a bit pedantic. I'm using the term* critique group *here on purpose, to differentiate these from* workshops. *Though they sound similar, they are two very different things. When I hear writers talking about getting feedback from their group, I assume they mean a group of writers they expect to critique their work. This is a session, or a process. A workshop, to me, is a class of some sort, structured to help a writer learn something specific.*

· · ·

I HAVE mentors who encourage the practice of using critique groups, and others who most expressly do not. I, being persnickety and obtuse, or any of a few other potentially gnarly adjectives, have a slightly different take on the whole thing.

First and foremost, as well as most relevant to this volume, I think the value of a critique group depends on whether you're working on short stories or novels.

Putting novels through a critique group always ends badly, even if the author doesn't know it will—or *especially* because the author doesn't know it will. This is at least partially because the new author invariably sends said novel through the group a chapter at a time, generally because they don't write faster than that and also probably because they are using the group's meeting date as a de facto deadline creator.

Deadlines are great, but there are better ways to skin that cat.

I mean, the pure drudgery of the timeline of a novel written as a chapter a month should be enough to send you running from the group's meeting room.

The real problem with novels in critique groups, though, is that there is no way I, or anyone else, can say anything useful about a novel they read a chapter a month. That's not how stories work. I don't judge a five-course meal by going to a restaurant for one dish the first of every month, and I don't watch a movie by taking in a scene every so often, either.

It just can't be done.

For short stories, though, I'm totally up with using critique groups to improve my writing—assuming I've got the right frame of mind, anyway. Like almost everything else good and holy, the value of critique groups is hidden in plain sight, but without the right mindset I'll miss it. When that happens, I'll get myself as gummed up as a Möbius strip in a peanut butter factory.

So how do I look at things the right way?

Well, let's start with the wrong way, and work ourselves to it.

THE WRONG MINDSET

Most writers think of their critique groups as if they are buddy mechanics who work at an auto shop.

They want advice about what's wrong with their car so they can then take it back to their own garage, make a few tweaks, and have it revving and ready to rumble a week later. In return they agree to spend time helping other writers fix their own cars.

As I used to say at my day job, that sounds wonderful in a conference room.

Alas, though, everything about this is wrongminded.

Let's start with the obvious: If I want someone to tell me what's "wrong" with my manuscripts, I can find beta readers who will be happy doing that without requiring me to reciprocate. All I have to do is ask.

This asking can be daunting. I remember it. Really, I do. Especially for new and fragile writers who haven't completely come out of the closet as writers.

The people I could ask were usually my friends.

What if they say no? Or what if they say yes, then read this precious baby of mine—this thing I think includes all my innermost thoughts—and decide they hate me?

Worries spin out of control for the normal person, and we writers are often far more susceptible to letting our imaginations run wild than the average bear. It's an oddly tough thing, to reveal to other people that I'm a person who is trying to tell stories. So much easier to just join with a few others who are also flailing around and dealing with their own insecurities.

But, yes, I can always find people to read my work without having to reciprocate.

That means I don't join a critique group to receive feedback.

In fact, when I do join a feedback group, I try to develop that muscle that lets me ignore most of what I hear. This is harder than it might sound, but I do it because another wrongminded thing about this approach is that the feedback I've received from critique groups has almost always been unhelpful. Worse, unless I am strong enough to ignore most of it, I've found it can do real damage.

This is because, as an extremely large rule of extremely large thumb, critique groups tend to be full of people who do not yet know how to write—but are often able to hum a few bars with the best of them. Did you feel weird about the idea of being an auto mechanic for a day up there in my opening to this chapter? If so, why do you feel differently about learning craft from the uninitiated?

Poorly targeted commentary can blunt a writer's advancement more than anything else, and feedback in critique groups is often poorly targeted because its providers are writers, and budding writers at that, not readers.

Yes, there is a difference.

And even in the unlikely event a new writer can provide feedback as readers (they do exist), members of your group are unlikely to represent your actual readers.

Perhaps they're not steeped in the genres you're writing in, or they read for character while you're more plotty, or they don't like vampire stories, or they simply can't overcome a social or political construct you've included in your work, or...well, the situations are infinite.

But, Ron, I can hear you say, these are all such great people!

We're all trying to learn together. Camaraderie! Solidarity!

We have to work with what we've got!

And, yeah, I love being with writers. It's fantastic. But there are ways to do this without cutting into each other's work. Go get dinner or have a drink. If you've got a sweet tooth, stop off at the local Dairy Queen and chat over ice cream. Whatever works. My very best writer friend ever came from a shared critique group, after which we would spend a couple hours getting dinner and dreaming of what it meant to write. Social contact with writers is a fantastic way to feed the fire inside you—and a fantastic way to learn about the business world of being a creative.

But I'm talking about the critique aspect of it—the literal ability of these people to dig into your work. As wonderful as all these people are—and critique groups really are almost always chock-full of wonderful, giving people—it's best to assume they cannot help you fix your work.

No one can tell you how to fix *your* story other than yourself.

So, no—joining a critique group so someone will fix your work is the wrong way to go.

THE RIGHT MINDSET

All the above being true, I *have* used such groups in the past and I've never failed to get something from them.

How so?

Well...I go into it with a very explicit mindset, which I will state here in its most combative form: *I do not care if I help the other writers in the critique group.*

That sounds the littlest bit abrasive, doesn't it?

Putting it that way makes my own skin crawl just a bit. I'm not insane enough to state it that way all the time. I don't make a habit of saying it that way out loud for fear of making people think I'm a selfish psychopath—which I'm not. Or at least I don't think I am. I think I'm generally approachable and quite open to helping other people—and when I'm in a critique group I partici-pate in good faith, using my skills as best I can to *try* to help them.

I have come, however, to accept the fact that their learning is on them.

They have to do the work.

They have to see things in their own fashion.

I really can't help them in the way they want to be helped because I am not them.

Still.

It's that don't-care part, right?

Reading my framework, well, it feels so sharp and so dismissive. It sounds like I'm giving the back of my hand to the other writers in any group, and selfishly stealing away with all the goodies.

Perhaps I should soften it to: *I can support other writers, but I know I can't help them with their craft.*

This works better when I'm talking to others, at least.

I'm rooting for these other writers, after all—there's nothing more enjoyable than seeing a friend or acquaintance take big steps up in their competence. If a fellow writer gets something valuable from a comment of mine, that's great. But, in general, I think most every writer is better off ignoring at least 95% of my input about their story.

The good ones (the "real" writers, to be pretentious here) will go on regardless.

HOW A CRITIQUE GROUP CAN MAKE YOU A BETTER WRITER

There is only one reason to be in a *critique group*: To get your hands on as many raw manuscripts as possible.

I learn by doing, after all.

I learn to tell stories by telling them myself—which is really what I'm doing when I read another person's work and make suggestions. Whether purposeful or not, I'm bringing *my* voice and *my* sensibility to pages someone else wrote. I can pretend to be neutral by trying to help the other writer's voice come through —but my realistic chances of being able to do that are slim to none. Instead, when I dig into someone else's manuscript, I acknowledge that I'm divining how *I* would do things differently.

In other words, I'm simulating an environment where I am telling that story.

I'm trying to make my own writing better, right?

If I'm not helping myself get better, I'll not show up to the critique group.

The whole point here is that this environment—a critique group where manuscripts are almost certainly not ones I'll consider to be "finished" (or "good" if I want to get pushy)—is a tailormade learning environment for a self-motivated writer. A pile of manuscripts I can deconstruct to my heart's content is the world's best simulation model. Each one sits there as a thought experiment—as an exercise for my mind.

And simulations are a great way to speed up learning.

I mean, it's a freaking goldmine.

THE PROCESS

I used to think that the process of deconstructing a story was so elemental that it didn't need to be discussed. That was before I started listening to writers. Now I realize that, as a collective, writers are like everyone else. We only go halfway.

By that, I mean most writers seem to think about breaking down a story as if it were a Seek and Find where their primary goal is to pick out flaws and hold them up to the light for all to see. That's all good and well, but it's also stopping way too early. That alone is not going to help my writing. Speaking for myself, anyway, the process has three steps:

1. Identify flaws.
2. Identify why the flaw is there…find where it was created and how it manifests itself.
3. Determine how I would write the story to remove the flaw, and then actually envision the change.

Most writers stop at #1, a few go onto #2, but almost no one goes to step #3.

THE VALUE OF TWO

You can, of course, do this all by yourself. Most of us do. Writing is an independent thing, and we get used to doing everything all by ourselves.

But a few years back my daughter, Brigid, and I attended a workshop that was predicated on writing short stories for anthologies, and as part of the process we'd receive a pile of some 250 manuscripts at a time. We decided we would get together and deconstruct them all—which we proceeded to do. We talked only about other people's stories, because there was a rule against talking about our own, and because, repeat after me, we know we can't really help each other. But we went through every manuscript in the pile, taking maybe 5-10 minutes each to look at story structure and characterization and whatever else struck our minds.

This takes learning to a new level.

Merely being expected to have a deep conversation about every story meant I couldn't shirk my work. Without the account-ability of talking to Brigid I would do a half-assed job of analysis, hence get step #1 wrong. And I learned a lot more by having a second point of view available to act as a sounding board. Some-times I miss things, you know? Sometimes Brigid came up with something that made me think about a work differently than I originally did.

If you're going to play in a critique group, I recommend you find a partner, and get to work.

This can be a bit of effort.

If you have ten people in your group, and everyone submits something, that means you're going to have eight stories to talk through every cycle. Multiply that by only five minutes each and you've got a 40-minute conversation. Ten minutes apiece says you need to tack on an hour and a half each session simply for the *conversation.*

But remember the goal. I want to make my own writing better, and this step turns the Critique Group into a Workshop.

BACK TO THE PROCESS

Partner or not, the process breaks into three segments:

1. What did I think of the work? What did I love? What went clunk? Did the writer achieve what they were trying to achieve, and do I like that? Were there other opportunities here? Would I have told a different story, and if so, what story would that have been?

2. I'll dig into the guts of the manuscript, sometimes laying out the plot in 7-point structure or thinking through the approach the writer took with information flow, or try/fail cycles, or validation scenes. What feels rushed? What's missing? Did the writer spend my time wisely? Occasionally I'll go down to specific phrases and words if I need to decide where a problem might be best addressed. Where is the writing weak, and why? Where did I lose attention?

3. I'll think through things I would do—this is where working with a partner can be valuable in understanding why I say one writer is so rarely able to really advance another. It was interesting to see how Brigid's approach would be different from mine.

This last bullet—thinking about how I would do something different from what was on the page is an important point. Sometimes—especially if I feel a manuscript is flawed in ways I get deeply interested in or if I think my solution is particularly tricky —I'll even go as far as to rewrite big portions of the manuscript.

That rewrite isn't useful as actual work, of course.

I can't publish it, and I don't ever share it with anyone, not even the writer.

Why would I? I'm not trying to help the writer in question at this point.

At this point, the writer in question has no bearing in the conversation at all. In fact, if I gave my work to them and they took it, I'd be breaking their voice and inserting mine, which is the definition of hurting a writer. Full admission here, when I was a younger writer, I'd do that—it was wrong then, too, I just didn't know it.

So, instead, I'm being selfish here.

At this point I'm trying to answer the question of *how I would write it*. So, when I picture or create the change I'm thinking about, I bring the learning full circle.

The magic sauce in using critique groups this way is that these manuscripts are ones I've never seen before—unlike my own, which I'm so close to I can't see them fairly. I've got no skin in the game, and hence am free to think outside the box.

That's what makes it a simulation, I suppose.

And that's what makes it all work.

The best times, of course, are when I find stories in a critique group that I wouldn't change at all. But, even then, I'll jump into the manuscript to look at how and why something really worked —especially those pieces that take great risks.

I do this often with published stories from my favorite authors.

I'd guess you do that, too.

The questions then become: How did they pull that off? Where did they set the hook? How did the writer leave me totally delighted?

SO, WHAT CRITIQUE GROUP SHOULD I JOIN?

The goal is to find a group that creates manuscripts of a class you can use to get better. They need to be good enough that you can see a story in them. After that, it's all fine.

That's the magic, really.

This is probably the reason critique groups I've been in have worked better when their members are at a similar level to me. These groups create manuscripts filled with the kinds of mistakes I make but are not manuscripts that I created.

Weird, right?

This is not about whether a writer is published or not.

It's simply where they are in their learning curve.

Do they know the basics? Do they seem to understand story structure, even if they can't always pick it out? Do they have a sense for setting and plot? Have they been working long enough to have developed at least some element of their voice?

If those things align with my own status, I think I've hit paydirt.

If you buy my take here, this is also why a real writer (as differentiated from a hobbyist) will likely "outgrow" a group. Or better stated, it's why a writer might stop feeling a group is helping them. A beginner can learn a lot from other beginners (we've all been there), but that will change. A writer who is truly working to get better will move on from a critique group when their learning gets stalled—and that will happen when the group's manuscripts don't present enough of a challenge to them. That writer may not even be able to describe why they aren't happy with the group, but they will leave rather than stagnate.

In other words, if the group I'm in is submitting manuscripts I can learn from, I'll stay, otherwise, I'm gone.

It's a theory, anyway.

What Is a Career?

COMEDIAN CHRIS ROCK has an amazing bit on the difference between a job and a career. I'm guessing you can still find it on YouTube or some other video platform. It's four or five minutes long, so if you have a moment, you should look it up. The gist of it is this: The difference between a career and a job is their relationship to time. When you have a career there is never enough time for you to finish everything you want to accomplish, but time on a job moves at a pace that gouges your soul.

I thought about this when a writer I admire wrote something about running out of time to chase dreams, noting that it can become too late to have a career.

I suppose that's true.

The word *career* carries the connotation of both a long timeframe and of supporting a person financially. I suppose that's true, too. At least the timeframe part. But I don't like adding the financial aspect into it. I think that makes the definition too small.

Rock's bit made me think about what it means to have a writing career, and specifically a career writing short stories.

Is that even possible? I thought.

Can you have a career in a field even if you never work at it "full time"?

Yes. I think so.

In fact, I'd guess a lot of writers have had careers that never resulted in them completely supporting their lives in the financial sense. Does that mean their career was less worthy than those who did it full time?

I don't think so.

If I dwell on financial success, or raw productivity, then these part-time careers were likely less successful than others, but I can't say their careers were less worthy or less valuable. Who is to say, after all, what the value of that career was to that writer when simply the act of writing those short stories may well have been the one true thing in their life—the one personal thing that fed their sense of self-worth and allowed them to accept the rest of the crap that fell on them?

Maybe I'm just spinning too fine of a thread here.

I don't know.

In my book, though, you can have a career writing short stories, even if you never make your living with them. You can have a career writing short stories (or novels for that matter, or poetry, or limericks, or…) by simply applying your time to pursuing it. The only real requirements are that this pursuit fills your soul, that you create something, and that you don't stop.

And that, if for some reason you do quit, well, then the only requirement is that you come back.

Personally, I'd say I've quit writing twice in my life (or three times if you include dropping it after school). One of those times —this last one—was "justified" in that I made an actual choice to focus my energy elsewhere. The other time I simply let the weight of the grind wear me away until I just never made back it to the keyboard.

But that's something about a career—which maybe I'm guilty of conflating with a calling.

It will call you back.

So, the only requirement to having a career is that you answer the call.

Rewriting

ONE OF HEINLEIN'S oft-quoted rules was that a writer should never rewrite unless at editorial request.

Never has a single commandment caused such a ruckus.

Sometimes I think he put it that way simply to create a stir. What exactly is rewriting, after all? Did Heinlein just dash off a draft and mail it to editors fresh off the old typewriter?

Seriously?

What about typos? What about when a story jumps the shark? What if I see a mistake and know how to fix it?

I mean, not every accident winds up with peanut buttery goodness in my chocolate.

Like most things, my experience sits on the edge of this thinking.

My first drafts tend to be "cycled," meaning I'm cycling back as I complete the draft. Adjusting things. Picking different words as I find the story. And even in stories I outline, there are always newly identified parts that get unearthed in the drafting.

That said, I'm an Anne Lamott follower when it comes to my first drafts in that they are intended to be just the littlest bit shitty. What is "Dare to Be Bad," after all, if not an acknowledgement that sometimes you're going to suck?

My first drafts tend to be discovery drafts—meaning I'm still finding the story and, most often, what that story means.

The second draft is for making changes I need to bring that story out from the morass I first created. The third draft, if necessary, is then mostly about making sure everything hangs together. I admit that I tend to throw away a lot of words.

That said—once I've gotten that far, I need to keep my hands off it.

I've done my best, anyway. So why revisit it?

My only caveat is that on occasion I've gone back to a story after several years have passed and, with totally fresh eyes and perhaps more skill today than yesterday, been able to make it work.

So, should you rewrite?

Probably a little.

But remember this is supposed to be sustainable. Sooner or later, crashing your head against the same rock over and over again is going to hurt.

Better a new work than an old rock.

EDITORIAL CHANGES

Then there is the rewriting that even Heinlein accepted: Editorial request.

Occasionally an editor will contact me for changes they feel are needed. Sometimes that request is "do this and I'll license your story," and other times it's a more open-ended "I liked this, but I had troubles here and there. If you'd like another try, I'll be happy to look at it again."

Do as you will, of course, but remember this is your decision.

Sometimes it's better to not be published.

Once a story is accepted, there could be another round of suggestions—specifically as regards to copyediting. These final directions from an editor can range from literally nothing, to light line edits or requests for heavy changes. Regardless, it's important to retain the idea that this is always your call.

It's your career, right? Your work.

That said, it's also true that processing the manuscript needs to be a "win-win or no deal" thing, meaning that if an editor asks for changes and I don't like those changes I have to be free to—professionally—reject them. Likewise, if I agree to make changes, then later argue about them to the point where I might eventually pull a story, the editor is well within their rights to get more than a bit chuffed.

It's Got a Beat, Jim!

AFTER YEARS of thinking about my own work, I've come to the idea that having a career in this field is about finding and maintaining my beat. By that I mean understanding whatever's going on around me, and then configuring my life around how it relates to creating stories.

My family is important to me.

I was lucky enough that when I had a day job it was more fulfilling than not, and its environment was filled with people I admired and enjoyed being around. Of course, it also brought in the money I needed to, as my grandfather once would say, keep the lights on and the cows fed.

Different times in my life resulted in the world demanding different things from me, so I was constantly required to adjust the way I used my time.

Psychologically, this is tough for a writer trying to get into the game or to stay in it. All the cool people were publishing all the time, right? And all my friends were constantly leaving me in their dust. No matter where I was, I wanted to be doing more. No matter how much I finished, I felt like I was falling farther and farther behind.

And that's a death spiral.

Really, it is.

It feels claustrophobic in the way I imagine drowning might feel.

Which is why I've sometimes said that success in creating a career in this world is so much about keeping your mind in the right emotional state to be able to do your best work. When things are going great, this is easy-peasy. But life isn't always great, and sometimes the only way to stay sane is to learn whatever trick you can learn that allows you to control whatever few things you can, then keep coming to the page at whatever rate your world will allow.

Through my life, the ability to find those tricks comes as seeing that my work will always have a beat.

This beat is the pace, given how I live at the time, at which I can finish things.

LET me talk about word count for a moment.

There are people who sit down at the keyboard and can simply spill out thousands of words of publishable fiction on command.

They exist.

Or at least they *say* they exist. I've met a few, anyway.

I do not like those people.

Not much, anyway. Not in that moment I hear them talking about it.

Oh, sure, they may *seem* like normal and even sane people when I meet them. They may seem likeable and wholesome, but deep inside I am certain their basement houses a shriveled, Dorian Gray-like painting of...I don't know...Shakespeare or Asimov... covered by some dusty old cloth.

Ain't natural, I say.

But then what *is* natural?

How fast *should* I write?

When I was a baby writer, I gagged to hear professionals say they could finish entire stories in a single night—which at 3,000-7,000 words meant you had to be typing pretty damned fast. I pictured manic-haired mad scientists crashing fingers across the keyboard so fast smoke would rise, then throwing their heads back in ecstasy as they finished.

These days I understand.

Speed is a muscle that's part freedom from concern, part knowledge, and part immersion.

When I'm on a roll now—when I leave myself free to make mistakes, and allow myself to be vulnerable enough to tap into the characters on the page, and when I can make myself enjoy those characters and the situations I've put them in—I can do 1,000 words or more in an hour that are, if not publishable, at least not "bad."

The problem, however, is that I do not always leave myself free to make mistakes and I do not always tap into my characters.

It turns out that I am a human being.

On good days the air is sweet. I find it easy to commune with these characters of mine and suddenly words fly off my fingertips like they are sliding through butter. The bad days, though, words that should be flying in formation simply get clogged in the drain. Goodbye 1,000 words an hour, hello early pangs of writer's block.

Here's a thought, though.

What if word count isn't the point?

When we are writing, we think about productivity as hourly or daily words because words are generally easy to count. Every writer I know can tell you how many words they can produce in an average hour or day or week, and if you talk to enough of them, you'll find that pace varies from person to person. Some get a couple hundred words an hour, some a thousand or more.

This is fine.

When you look at their careers you'll see they're all prolific— meaning they are all publishing or at least finishing work routinely.

That last bit is the entire point, right?

If you're in this for the long haul—if you plan to be working in the field for years and years—the right lens to view things through is sustainability.

When I first thought that word—*sustainability*—it kind of slapped me in the face.

That's why I'm thinking about my "beat."

Sustainability, I've come to think, is about finding the natural beat inherent in your life situation, and then committing to it. Sure, I can write 10,000 words in a day if I need to. And in special situations that's fun as hell.

But I can't do it every day.

That's not sustainable.

Better, really, to think of stories.

Writers count words, after all. Readers count stories.

I'm willing to bet there has never been a person in the history of human creation who, as they read anything at all, has ever really worried about how many words the scribe wrote on any particular day.

The story is all that matters.

Can I do one in a week?

Two weeks?

It's all good. Whatever that rate is—in terms of stories, be they novels or short stories or anything else—is my beat.

And every beat is acceptable—as long as you're adult about it.

When you find your beat, hit it.

That's sustainability.

** ASIDE: I find it fascinating how many ways lifetime writers find to count words. And, yes, I do it too. I am a writer after all. My own fashion, these days, is to split my count into "New Words" and "Recycled Words." For example, this chapter is just north of 1,000 words—so when I wrote the first draft, I credited myself with 1,000 new words, but when I did my second pass, I credited them as 1,000 recycled words. I do this to remind myself that I want to be creating words fresh—and I've learned I need to hold myself accountable in that fashion. Other writers have different psychological needs, I guess. There is no wrong way. Just remember, though, the real point is still to get works done, not just words.*

Finding Your Beat

I HAVE DISCOVERED A SECRET FORMULA, which I will now pass on to you: My beat—stories/week or stories/month—is defined by the average amount of time I can spend writing over that time, divided by the average length of the stories I write.

Amazing, right?

You can send my Nobel Prize to my dad. I'll work on my acceptance speech next week, thank you very much.

LIFE WILL NOT COOPERATE, though. Which means my beat will sometimes just up and change on me without any warning at all.

There are times when things get intense, and the world gets so large that it bleeds into every space my soul possesses. When that happens, time collapses—and even when there's breathing space the words won't come. That's all right, I tell myself.

Just breathe.

Writing may sometimes feel like life, but in reality, only life is life.

When life is hard, it's okay to let go of my words.

I want to be real with my writer self, though. I don't want to pretend.

While sustainability is not about pushing through at all costs, it *is* about being honest with myself and configuring my life (however it is) around the idea of getting work done. When I do that, I have that natural beat—that pulse, that natural cycle of production that (I hate to break it to you) will still vary, depending.

To be sure, I've been a lot of different writers in my time.

- The 4:30-to-6:30 AM writer with a day job
- The "grab 15 minutes where I can" writer
- The "I just can't" writer
- The "seat-of-my-pants-er"
- The "planner"
- The all-points-in-between writer

When I was a 4:30-6:30 AM writer, I could get a short story finished in one or two weeks. When I was a "15 minutes where I can" writer, I was slower. As a planner, I was faster at the keyboard, but slower overall because I spent more time planning than was perhaps necessary. As a seat-of-my-pants-er I'm blazingly fast at the keyboard but can be wasteful overall as I go down blind alleys.

Today I'm a "full-time" writer, so my beat is considerably higher—but I'm also a primary caregiver to an elderly parent, which means that "full-time" can be dramatically cut at a moment's notice.

Ultimately, it's my job to take control of the parts of life that are available to me and use them as I will. There is a strange beauty hidden inside this idea: When I'm working along with life, giving myself to a sustainable writing cycle can make me happy, which then adds flavor to the rest of who I am.

My body tells me when I'm in the right state.

When I am on my beat, finishing a writing session feels good —I know I've done something important to me, and now that I've given myself that space I can allow myself to do the rest of what I want to do without being concerned for shortchanging my writing. When I'm using my time properly (dangerous word, that *properly*, right?) I am happy. When I am using my time properly, I am a better husband and a better father and a better friend.

When I give my brain its writing time, it rewards me in strange ways.

My stray thoughts throughout the day might play with a plot point I'm not happy with. Or, in the middle of a business meeting, for example, I might find the reason my protagonist isn't doing what I want her to do. As my life is today, I can tell when I'm in the right frame of mind because I wake up with pieces of projects floating in the grayness of my morning, and suddenly I can't get out of bed fast enough because I want to write them down.

Your mileage may vary here.

Everyone is different.

But for me there is a physicality to my day that, when I've used my time to its best capacity, makes me happy. For me, it's like the undercurrents of my brain are silently churning away, steadily writing, even when my body isn't.

Here's another interesting thing.

When I am in this mode, completing work in that sustainable way my life can support, I feel the stories come through me like they are imprinted in my blood, and in those times—those glorious days when that blood is on fire and words simply spill out faster than I can capture them—all of life itself is beautiful.

Being Cool with Your Beat

BUT WHAT IF my beat is only a paltry short story a year?

Hmmm.

If that's a true thing—if you really cannot find enough time to produce faster, then that's fine. All you can do is your best. There was a time in my life where I was fine with not producing anything. If, as a good-faith adult, you can look at yourself in the mirror and know you're doing the right thing, then the ultimate challenge is to find a way to be happy with that one story a year.

Be responsible.

Hold yourself accountable for the truth.

When your life changes, and you are ready to come back, be real about that rate and make changes.

Otherwise, perhaps you might need to assess if this writer career is really what you want.

Go back to the Chris Rock definition and decide if you have a career or a hobby.

There is no shame in writing as a hobby. None at all.

Don't let it eat you up.

IF YOU ARE a new writer this may be the first time you've thought about structuring your life around a beat in this way.

When I was a new writer, I was generally dissatisfied with the idea that I could write "only" two hours a day. I wanted more, but I had that 10-12 hour day job, and a wife and a kid with school plays and I would see other writers in my same phalanx who seemed to be writing so much quicker than I did and their stories were showing up in magazines and anthologies while mine were simply getting enough form rejections to plaster my walls with.

In those days I would listen to professionals talk about their own processes, and I would be jealous, thinking such thoughts as *Well, Mr. Professional Writer sitting there so high on your pedestal, if I had all day to create stuff, I could do that too.*

My jealousy could get pretty ugly if I let it.

Creatively, sometimes that dissatisfaction would show up in my work.

It was so easy to forget that this writing gig is supposed to be fun—that creation of art is supposed to be joyful at its core. Perhaps that sounds the tiniest bit indulgent or Bohemian, but I find it important to keep in mind that writing stories is *supposed* to be fun.

Hard at times, certainly.

Frustrating at times also.

But writing is supposed to fulfill my life, not auger my psyche into the ground.

Still, when things aren't coming off the "production line" quickly enough, I feel pressure building, and if I let it go too long my writer brain will get constipated, and suddenly this creation of stories becomes so much like work that it makes me grumpy.

As I noted before, life is too short to be grumpy all day, and so much of a writer's career is about keeping themselves in an emotional state to simply do good work.

Blah, bleeping blah, blah, blah.

HERE'S PROBABLY the most important thing I've learned when it comes to finding and maintaining my own beat: Comparing myself to other writers at any time in my life has never gone well.

That includes comparing myself to myself.

You know what I mean, right?

Maybe last month I did a great job of using what time I had, and I had more time than usual.

Or maybe I was just writing something that came so naturally that the words flowed like magic. Maybe today I'm doing true exploratory "pants-ing" and that means I'm going to write a lot of words that won't fit—so at the end of the day I'm back to square one.

If I'm gunked up today, looking at how my work was a month ago is not going to help.

Just like casting a jealous eye to all of my friends who are busy releasing new stories is not going to help either.

When I am unhappy with my work, I need to look within.

Am I giving myself the proper time within the context of everything else that's going on?

If I am being successful—if I'm giving myself that time—am I bringing myself to the page in the proper frame of mind?

Am I having fun?

Why not?

———

THAT SAID, I think most of us grossly underestimate our ability to create words rapidly.

The Anthology workshop I often attended ran on the beat of a short story every week—meaning the 6,000-word assignment is given on day one, and then is due a single week later.

That happened six times in a row—so, six stories in six weeks.

If you are an established writer, my guess is that you'll mostly likely not blanch at that idea at all, but as a young writer I found that concept daunting.

Something magical happens when I'm on my beat, though. My brain settles.

Words come more cleanly.

I click into characters more rapidly, and when my session is done I can look back and suddenly realize that ... *hey, I can actually write quickly!*

Or, if this is your first time getting serious about giving yourself such a space, you might well look back on what you've done and realize that ... *hey, I can actually structure my life in such a way that I can write that often!*

As I write this, I am coming off a very intense period of my life.

Like everyone else on the globe I've been living through an unhappy pandemic, and processing several of the world's problems as they unfold in front of me. On the personal front I've been dealt a hand that includes non-Covid health issues for both of my parents, as well as my wife.

I made decisions over this time that caused my beat to be reduced so far that, if pressed, I would say that I quit creating words for a time.

That sensation of comparing myself to other writers during this period was strong.

Looking back on it, I know this much: I made my choice, and to be honest I am happy with having made it.

But I promised myself a long time ago that I wasn't going to deceive myself.

When I eventually recognized my ability to handle daily life had started getting better, when overall, in fact, I thought things were finally getting pretty good, I looked at myself and knew the time had come. I needed to hold myself accountable for coming back to the keyboard. I needed to find a new beat, and I needed to be cool with that.

Being more experienced about these things now, I knew how to do it.

Here's the secret: Start small. Give yourself to the work. Believe in yourself—that the work will be "good," whatever "good" is.

For me "starting small" meant asking myself to be happy with 250 words a day until I finished something.

That felt paltry.

Only one page.

No real writer does just a page a day.

But that's not true. I knew it wasn't true because Tobias Buckell, a writer who'd grown up just a little younger than me, reported that as he came out of a pandemic funk, he'd gotten himself jump-started by being happy with 250 words a day. If it was good enough for Toby, it was good enough for me.

So that's where I was. Giving myself to the work for 250 words a day.

Minimum.

Pretty soon it was 500 words a day, then 900, then 1,000.

Along the way I gave myself some other deadlines. For example, I found a project that made me drop words on my website every day.

It built up my muscles, you know. Got me used to hearing the clacking of the keyboard again and reminded me what the rhythm of fingers flowing across the keyboard felt like.

Before you know it, I'd completed a short story. And then another.

A novel came out.

Then two more short stories.

And another.

Then this manuscript appeared almost out of thin air.

Next thing you know, I was—once again—dancing to the drum of my own beat.

Speed vs. Quality, Part I

THE READER DOES NOT CARE how long it took to complete the masterpiece they are in the process of devouring. This is true when *I* read. It is true when *you* read.

Seriously.

Nobody cares. How long. It took. You to. Write this. Story.

This means it is completely fine to have written that story in a week. Or a day. Or maybe four hours. Really, it's okay. Oh sure, you can also spend months going back over and over work if that really pleases you. But it is not necessary.

The reader does not care.

I have on several occasions written short stories in just a few hours.

"Yes," I hear you say, "but are these stories any good?"

This is the response I get most anytime I talk about creating words quickly. People focus only on time spent and ignore the idea that letting oneself write quickly is a great way for a writer to find a way into the creative side of their brain. They accentuate this idea that just pounding out words is inherently bad.

Sigh.

When you're a newer writer, and sometimes even when you're a more established one, this question can really get your knickers up in knots.

"Are these stories any good?"

First, let me ask: Can you handle the truth?

Because the fact is that, yes, some of the stories I write quickly are not very good.

It's true. Sometimes they're rushed. Sometimes I miss entire scenes that are necessary, and that I don't realize I've missed until a Hugo Award winning editor points it out...eep!

That's life. It happens to us all.

But in many cases—or at least a considerable number of them —short stories written quickly are fantastic. I've noted elsewhere that the Anthology workshop I often participated in required stories to be written in a week, and several of them went on to fill recommended reading lists, receive nominations, and win awards.

Some wound up in Year's Best collections.

This is one of the more important learnings a new writer can have, really: Trying to answer the question of what is "good enough" in a world of artistic endeavor can melt your brain.

Seriously, no one cares how long it takes you to write a piece.

The confidence, however, that comes from realizing it's *actually possible* to write an award-quality story in a week or less can lead to a greater sense of freedom and a more carefree feeling of audacity—two traits that are absolutely attractive for writers.

Two traits it takes for a writer to leave themselves free to be themselves.

Speed vs. Quality, Part II

ANOTHER FACT IS, no matter who you are, it's almost guaranteed that your work is not where you want it to be. I know mine has never been where I wanted it to be. Even in the good moments, I've known I wanted to be a better storyteller. Sometimes I don't know what my work is (I am a suspect judge of my own work). It could be that my work is actually flawed, and I don't know how to fix it (my craft hasn't been honed), or it could be any one of a hundred different things.

Every writer I know—from newbie to curmudgeonly vet—is trying to get better.

Still, when you are new, there's something mystical about the learning curve.

Here's a truth, though: The *fastest* way to learn how to tell stories is to tell a lot of stories. If you don't see that clearly, let me state the counter rule: The *slowest* and *most painful* way to learn is to keep working on the same story over and over and over.

Sure, you *can* learn either way. But writing stories "quickly" (whatever that means for you) means you're constantly moving forward.

So, tell the story you're working on now to the best of your ability, and then move on.

Several of my friends, for example, engage in a commitment to write a story a week for a year.

That's a powerful idea.

If a story you wrote in week one failed, you've got the learning from it. So go apply it to week two. Three months or a year later you might come back to that first story and know how to fix it, but for now you have other stories to make happen.

My favorite part of watching people do this is seeing the stories they write in these periods get accepted and then published. It always delights them—as if they find their success surprising. It does not surprise me, though. While at the week-long *Writers of the Future* workshop my first time (back in the late 1990s), I wrote eight stories in four days, and six of them eventually went on to be published. One of them missed a Hugo nomination by one vote and grew into a series of novels that still sell today.

(Story of my life, I tell you, story of my life)

So, yes, I learn more rapidly by doing new work than I do by treading back over old.

I think you will, too.

And yes, some of those stories are going to be absolutely fantastic.

Stalled Writers

Sometimes I get stuck. You know. Mired.

Not blocked so much as just stymied.

My head will be in the wrong place (Insert Kevin Costner's Crash Davis getting on my case and calling me Meat here).

I've been doing this for…a long time. In that span I've had cycles where I've been frozen in my thinking about whether I was good enough, and times when, no matter what I did, I've looked at the page and seen nothing but another form rejection coming.

Writing fiction is not for the faint of heart.

I need to bring audacity to the page. I need to find confidence to do my work—the audacity and the confidence to help me think that what I'm doing is worthwhile. If I don't have that confidence and audacity, it can be damned hard to make words do anything.

I think this is true of almost everyone—especially in the early stages.

Terms like *blocked* or *burned out* or *tired* or *useless* slip into conversations. The fact is that there are probably as many reasons a writer might be lacking that audacity as there are writers.

For example, I once listened in on a conversation with a writer who was bemoaning, as kindly as it's possible to do so, other writers who fall into what that writer called such self-loathing that they can't write. "I don't get it," that writer said. "I've never beat myself up like that."

"It's not self-loathing," I finally said, then went on to say that these writers aren't hating themselves, or even hating their work. Not really. Instead, they're just worried. Being a writer often means you're working without a net and without feedback. "Sometimes writers get to the point where they don't know if they're good enough," I said. "And they're alone, and all they see out in the world is this big sucky vat of sucking darkness that's draining their soul without giving them an ounce of feedback to let them ground themselves."

In cases like this, a writer can get so caught up in themselves that they just flail around and then eventually find themselves stagnating.

Here are a few examples of what I mean:

- If you are a brand-new writer, you might have flat-out no idea how to do the work, which is daunting.
- If you've been working for a while, you might be feeling the true grade of the mountain you're climbing, which is wearying.
- If you've had some success, you might be worried you can't duplicate your own accomplishments, which is scary as hell.
- If you've had friends succeed, you might think you'll never be able to match them, which can tie you up in so many awkward knots I prefer not to think about it.
- Or you might be just getting around to realizing that you'll never have a voice like Neil Gaiman's.
- Or … well, you get the idea.

Add in the pressures of work or family, or any of the things that can get into our heads to tell us we're no good, that we'll never make a difference, that no one would ever want to read something we wrote…well, those things are literally infinite.

To that I say this.

It's all right. Again, just breathe.

Find a moment, maybe just ten minutes even, and just let yourself make words.

Play a game with them, describe someone you love, then give yourself a reasonable deadline and write even more about them.

Make a story. Love that story for everything it is.

Then do it again.

It's okay.

Really it is.

Editors: Imagining Life on the Dark Side

IMAGINE you are the new acquiring editor of a reasonably sized magazine, and you love short stories to the maximum degree it's capable for any human being to love short stories.

You go into work the first morning and, whistling a jaunty tune, you arrive at the office ready for an exciting day of finding material for future issues. Since your publication is looking for short stories, you're always on the lookout for fresh voices, and since you're always on the lookout for these cutting-edge writers, your submission pile is open to the public. This means that when you arrive at your desk, the first thing you do is open your in-box to find fifty new manuscripts (which everyone in the industry affectionately or not so affectionately calls the "slush pile"). This is not unusual, of course. Your publication gets 1,500 submissions a month, so fifty is simply an everyday occurrence.

The good news of course is since we're talking about short stories, and since our definitions all suggest you can read these stories in a single setting, we will say the average time to get through a single story is a mere fifteen minutes. You pick the first one out of the inbox and dig in. Fifteen minutes later you've finished that story and determined it's not for you. You append a form rejection and send a note back to the writer saying thank you very much.

You're now done with one submission.

Outstanding!

You do this three more times, then note that an hour has passed.

You see where this is going, right?

At this pace completing those fifty manuscripts will take you twelve and a half hours, and that's not taking into account lunch, coffee, or any other issues that might arrive through the day.

Something's gotta give.

HAVING EDITED AN ANTHOLOGY NOW, I can say this.

Editing is a true skill and a real art form. Sure, there's craft to it. But the idea of supporting a writer from the editorial seat is interesting. It's very different from providing critique. Critique is about saying how I felt about something, Editing is about trying to get under the writer's skin and helping them say what they were trying to say—only better.

It's a very fine line.

My sweetie is literally a world-class copy editor who has worked for many of the top houses in the field. So, yes, I had a pretty high regard for the work of all the various types of editors when I started the process of co-editing *Face the Strange*, but to be put into the role and have to actually do the job served to raise my level of appreciation for them.

Reading Like an Editor

You probably have a day job, right? Family events to attend. Favorite teams to follow.

Well, editors have those, too, meaning the day-job thing in specific. Short fiction editors rarely do this as their primary gig, but they still need to put out a magazine on schedule. And that example of 1,500 manuscripts in a month isn't really exaggerated. An editor's workload can be intense. Their time really is like gold. It's almost embarrassing to admit how much more intense it is to read from the editorial seat than to read for pure joy.

When I read for joy, I'm looking for a way into every story.

I *want* to be hooked, and I'm willing to grab almost anything and run with it. But when I read as an editor, I suddenly found myself looking for a way out—any way out. "I've got 35 stories to finish by tomorrow," I thought. "How can I get this done?"

I think it's fair to say that a reader is thankfully oblivious to this.

But if you've been doing this writing gig for any amount of time, then at least intellectually you already understand the dynamic.

Until you get "stuck" with the work, though, you can't really feel the depth of an editor's pain, nor the uplifting joy that comes with finding something you absolutely love, as well as the weird juxtaposition of emotions that come from finding something you absolutely love but know you can't use.

Editorial decisions, it turns out, are hard.

HERE'S AN EXERCISE FOR YOU.

Simply pick up any collection or anthology of short stories you haven't read yet and give yourself a good-faith thirty or forty-five minutes to select three of them as a collection of your own.

Or, if you are a critique group person, do it with your next group of submissions.

Seriously.

Set a timer, preferably one that has an audible *tick tock*. Then make yourself do it.

It's an interesting exercise.

Where do you stop reading?

Why do you stop?

The Anthology workshop I often attended would dump a couple hundred manuscripts on me and give only a few weeks to build six anthologies of six different themes. I'm sure you can daydream other ways of putting yourself in the shoes of an editor like this, and all of them should work—so long as the basic situation results in a pile of manuscripts you need to go through in a limited amount of time.

Being an editor brought a lot into my writing that I thought I knew already but hadn't fully appreciated.

Things like: There are reasons openings are important. Make that first page pop. Make *something* interesting happen NOW. First sentences with hooks, and characters in settings with problems, and clean language and strong voice give stories early velocity. They help readers get going.

When you put yourself in editor mode, you quickly come to understand why the legends of editors rejecting manuscripts based on one paragraph exist.

There is only so much time in the day.

HERE'S ANOTHER POINT. One that I'll title: familiarity breeds excitement.

When I'm faced with that mound of work, and I come upon a piece by someone I'm familiar with and whose work I've enjoyed, or not enjoyed, I find it nearly impossible not to have preconceived feelings about that work. I will be rooting for that writer the minute I start, or be worried for them, or…whatever. When I run into those feelings, either positive or negative, I try to examine them, then put them in context of my own career.

When I was just starting to sell, Stan Schmidt, the *Analog* editor of the time, told me the worst thing I could do was to sell him one story. "I want to buy from someone whose name I eventually can put on the cover," he said. "I've been following you in the slush pile. I've been rooting for you because I know you're going to keep sending me stories." This feeling of excitement you get about a writer in your own slush pile is related to that idea. Editors of traditionally published magazines are rooting for you. They want to buy careers if they can. That's your goal. It's this aspect of expectation that is at the root of moving out of the slush pile into the "pro pile."

There's a bit to unpack in that comment.

It's easy, for example, to say a writer grabs attention by writing great stories—great openings with interesting events and a validation that punches really should win the day eventually. But Stan's comment carries something deeper, too. Woody Allen is credited with saying something like: 90% of success is simply showing up.

Which is, interestingly, also something like the equation for having a career.

I'VE LEARNED a few things while editing that inform my writing even today.

I have, for example, a deeper respect for the value of titles.

It was amazing how even fantastic stories were forgettable a day after I read them simply because their titles were bland. Reading the first sentence of one of those stories would bring it flooding back, but the titles wouldn't always work.

While writing, I've always "understood" that titles make a difference, and as a reader that's equally true. A great title all by itself makes me want to read the story. But when you're dealing with a couple hundred works and you're trying to keep them all separated in your mind, a bland title just makes everything fade. On the other hand, it was equally amazing to see how entire stories would come flooding back when the author selected the right title.

I loved that.

Titles, my friends. Don't shortchange them.

I also have a much greater appreciation for taking risks.

The manuscripts Brigid and I were looking at for *Face the Strange* were all submitted by hard-working writers, and as such were all structurally competent. You could read them easily, and they all had "proper" elements. Those things are important. But that's a very craft-laden view of the game. When I'm looking for memorable stories, though, I'm looking for things that take my breath away. In editing *Face the Strange*, Brigid and I ran into stories that were gently flawed, but whose ideas or voices were so strong we knew we had to publish them. One had an opening that was technically too slow, but that worked perfectly for the story. Another had pacing issues, but we *needed* it because the concept and the rest of its execution were too awesome to pass up.

The question we asked in these cases was "is the extra work worth it?"

And when the payoff was high, when the writer took bigger risks, the answer was almost always "yes."

In other words, if you're interesting, you can get away with anything.

I think I've heard that somewhere before.

Grin.

On the Term Slush Pile

THE TERM *SLUSH* *pile* is used to describe the mound of manuscripts that get sent an editor's way. It is an ugly-sounding term. Probably for good reason. Spend any time in newbie forums, and you'll read a wide array of ungainly work.

I have gotten into animated conversations with writers regarding the term.

It is bound to raise hackles, after all.

The slush pile is like a dumping ground. It brings to mind the image of an old 49er pulling a bucket of silty river sludge from a stream in hopes a few bits of gold would stand out. I see the miner's eyes, wild from the claim and his bristly beard haggard from too many nights sitting up guarding the perimeter.

The term is too vague, though. The slush pile actually has at least three gradients. If you are going to have a career writing short stories your first goal is to get out of the dregs of the first one, the primary pile where everything goes at first, and into a different class—what I'll call the *neo-pro pile*. This second group is where an editor puts the manuscripts they anticipate are going to be at least interesting. Perhaps this is because they've bought work from you before, or because they've simply been seeing your name on enough manuscripts that you're interesting, or they have met you in person, or...whatever. The point is that the editor already has a preconceived idea that they might want to publish your work.

Then there's the Nirvana that is the pro pile itself.

These are the manuscripts the editor *knows* are going to hold interest.

You can, of course, be rejected from any of those piles, but it's easy to see why the strata exists and what they mean.

In the old days these were three physical manifestations, three actual piles of envelopes. Today almost everyone uses electronic systems, and I imagine the triage of processing manuscripts is a little bit different in each office. But the concept remains.

There are ways to tell if you've moved up.

First and foremost, your rejections might start having comments attached to the boilerplate form. If you're a new writer submitting into the void, you'll get used to these templates. Then those comments might start coming from the editor themselves rather than from a first reader. Finally, you might get the notorious "personal rejection," which is a note that says no thanks, but includes comments from the editor, and often a request to see more.

Those are great moments.

** An aside: I remember sitting with Mike Resnick, who was also a prolific editor back when I was a baby writer. I was describing a personal rejection I had received from an editor—which was a matter of some joy to me at the time. He sat there with that smile he could get, and when I was done, he said, "You realize that the key word in the phrase* personal rejection *is* rejection, *right?"*

There are obvious reasons for this progression, and perhaps some that are not so obvious.

Editors really are rooting for you. They like being the person who buys a new writer's first story. Put yourself in their shoes, and you can imagine how that would feel. A certain gravitas comes with plucking the next hot new name out of the stream.

The different mindset between magazine editors and anthology editors can be an interesting study, too. Anthologies, especially theme anthologies, are often essentially one-hit wonders. Anthology editors generally know exactly what they're trying to build, and they look at a manuscript against that framework alone. Magazine editors have a new issue to fill every month or every quarter. So while they look at the material itself, they also are looking for writers they feel are going to be reliable.

The slush pile can be different in each situation.

To make it even more daunting, though, you should realize *there is no single pro pile.* Every editor is different, so climbing out of the open cesspool of slush in one editor's mind is not good enough. Then there's the fact that editors change seats.

Geez.

It's enough to drive me crazy.

That said—until we are *anticipated* by an editor, we all start in the big pool of primordial slush. There's no shame in this. Especially early in our careers, it has very little to do with the quality of our work and a lot to do with the fact that no one at the editorial shop knows us.

In my own view, though, I try hard to just assume I'm always at the bottom—that my work is always viewed on equal terms with every other writer out there.

Anthologies
and Magazines

IF YOU WANT to make headway with short stories, I'm sorry to say that you have to pay attention to markets—by that I mean magazines and anthologies. This might well be changing as I type. I'll talk about some folks doing interesting things with short stories in the independent ranks in the next section, but for now I suspect you'll find the headwinds of independently publishing short fiction quite hard to deal with in the early stages of your career.

Go ahead, though. Please do prove me wrong.

I'm rooting for you.

Anyway, here are a few notes regarding traditional markets for short fiction.

1. Reading the guidelines is important, especially for themed anthologies, but stretching the guidelines is often more important. Finding fresh or unusual takes on ideas inside a set of guidelines is often what makes a story stand out.

2. It's hard to stretch the guidelines in a way that works without first understanding those guidelines deeply. So, yes—read the guidelines carefully—then try to think right at the edges of them.

3. A magazine's guidelines are generally more about their brand than an editor's specific taste. Unless you just happen to know the editor, the only way you'll get a real sense of that taste is to read the magazine.

4. The stories with the freshest and most interesting takes are often things that come from places closest to the writer's heart. This can be scary.

5. The game can feel rigged, but it's not—except for where it is.

6. Writing is not a competition, except when it is.

7. Facts of business (space available, money available, inclusion of other writers, etc.) constrain the field, but are out of your control. Deal with it. This is the primary truth of writing in the traditional market.

8. Sometimes, especially in the case of anthologies, great stories get rejected because the editor received two or more of the same thing.

9. It helps to be a mind reader. Sometimes the guidelines aren't quite what the editor wanted. Yes, that sucks, but who said traditional publishing was easy?

Independent Publishing and the Short Story

DESPITE WHAT SOME PEOPLE SAY, you can have a career publishing short stories as an independent writer. They are a hard sell, yes, but in the sense that having a career is not all about whether that pursuit supports you full time, you can do it.

And who is to say, right?

Ultimate success for a writer in any form is always about building and growing a readership. And an independent writer's readership, whether large or small, can be avid. It is certainly possible an independent writer of short stories could eventually make a perfectly fine living with those short stories.

Arguably, it's already happening now.

To go back to the question I asked earlier, just what is a short story, after all?

My best-selling work is a series of novellas.

Are those short? At least one of the definitions I went over said they are. But I don't know, and I don't care.

All I care about is that readers are still finding them, still buying them, and still reacting well to them. That they were independently published does not seem to matter to anyone at all.

If you're a writer for whom awards matter, it's interesting to note that the independent market has made inroads in places like the Science Fiction Writers of America's Nebula Awards, too, which has seen independently published material make shortlists.

Who can tell what the future will bring?

IT'S an exciting time for the short story from the perspective of their use as a tool for a writer's business development. When I was a baby writer, for most short stories, their publication was essentially the end of their life. Sure, some stories would be reprinted in a collection or perhaps sold to a foreign market, but that's *some,* not *most.* Now, however, the possibilities are limited only by your mind, your time, and your...brazenness.

Independent writers are finding inventive ways to use great short stories to attract readers to their larger projects—which is the entire point, right? The ability to quickly interact with your readers in this fashion really hasn't existed until these modern times.

Short stories and novelettes can direct readers to longer series as well as serve to keep the appetites of current readers of those series whetted.

Independently published writers can also use short stories as attractive gifts for readers signing up for their newsletters— which is a great way to have a connection to people who are predisposed to love your work. You can find writers who use Patreon projects geared to the short story, or using those short stories to create award plateaus in various crowdfunding efforts.

Some writers use free stories to lure readers to their website, then make their work available directly from there.

Other writers are working their reader bases into the short stories as characters, which I admit I have not yet done but sounds like a whole lot of fun.

The ideas are endless.

So, my primary suggestion is—if you're willing to try new things—pour yourself into your creations, and just have fun promoting them.

I SHOULD POINT out one more value to the idea of independent publishing when it comes to the short story.

Relative to the idea of story structure itself, the act of publishing is a form of self-validation.

Publishing day comes with a sense of closure, right?

Even if sales don't immediately soar, the act of pushing the "publish" button means it's gone.

Done.

I do not need to go back and work on it again, because my work is now winging its way to whatever fate it has.

Time, then, to write something new.

Selling and Contracts

HAVING an editor say they loved your work so much they want to pay for the right to publish it will Never Ever Get Old. A letter of acceptance is like a hopped-up fan mail with the promise of a real check attached. It just doesn't get better than that. Any writer who tells you otherwise is either lying, or such a psychopath that perhaps you want to steer clear of them.

Don't get me wrong, though.

The thrill of seeing sales reports on an independent publishing chart is no different. That, also, never gets old. And meeting actual readers, and hearing excitement on their voices can be another equally thrilling sugar high. A great fan letter can set you to walking on clouds.

But I want to talk about selling short stories into the traditional market, now, so let's discount all the other things that can happen to boost your ego and settle into the bits of the business side of the industry that I think are most important to short story writers.

If you've sold work before, you'll know the basic drill.

CONTRACTS

At some point as the project gets put into the production pipeline, you'll receive a contract.

These can be gloriously intimidating moments for newly anointed writers and are sometimes not much better experiences for veterans. Read the contract. Understand the words there—all of them—and if you're not sure what you're agreeing to, questions are valuable. It's a very good idea at this point to talk to other writers. You will find them readily available to help.

On the positive side, short story contracts tend to be stream-lined—no more than a page or three on average.

Regardless, it is vitally important to understand you are leaving the world of artistry and creativity, and entering the cutthroat world of being a professional writer. You are now licensing your Intellectual Property, which means you will need to learn copyright law.

Might as well start now.

TO STATE THE OBVIOUS, let me start with the classic disclaimer that I Am Not A Lawyer. To that I'll add that if I *were* a lawyer, I would be an intensely horrible one. I do not have that kind of mindset and have no passion for that kind of attention to detail. Digging into arcane corners of the law would for me be like doing self-surgery.

I meant what I said, however: It is important that writers understand certain basics of copyright law, and even more important to understand when they don't understand.

Donald Rumsfeld's infamous quote comes to mind: *There are known knowns. These are things we know that we know. There are known unknowns. That is to say, there are things that we know we don't know. But there are also unknown unknowns. There are things we don't know we don't know.* Bumbling or not, that description of the situation certainly applies to an artist who is stepping into the murky world of the intellectual property industry.

Despite not being a lawyer, here are some things I think writers of short stories should keep in mind as they progress.

NEGOTIATIONS: It is important to understand that a contract is a negotiation, and in any negotiation I am able to ask for some-thing I want. The worst that can ever happen is that the publisher says no. Realize the editor in question *wants to publish my work,* and that no one is going to walk away from a deal simply because I asked for something that they weren't planning on giving me. Their response might be "no, and that is a deal breaker," but that's okay. It simply means I am going to have to decide if I can live without my request.

If I cannot live without it, that means I should decline the contract.

The whole point of a contract is to define a situation in which both parties are happy, or at least happy enough. It's important to see the long game here because once I sign the contract I'm going to live with the results. It is far better that my property remains unpublished, than for it to be published in a way I will regret in the future.

Those words *regret in the future* are important to me because this is my work.

I am the artist.

That means *I* get to be the one who defines what I will regret.

There are as many ways to look at this as there are people. *I* might regret giving away or underselling derivative licensing fees, whereas *you* may regret allowing translations or not having control of some specific formatting that you used in the manuscript. *You* might regret giving away a free option (which I'll get to in a moment), where *I* may just shrug my shoulders and not fret it at all.

This is your career.

Assuming you understand the deal, there are no right and wrong answers.

There is only what you feel is good for you.

A contract is a negotiation. Treat it that way.

RIGHTS LICENSED: This is probably the most important

section of all, and unfortunately it is also probably the most complex.

Read the contract.

Understand the rights the publisher is asking for.

Here is where you should really dig into copyright law. I say that because the number of ways you can license your intellectual property are bounded only by your ability to think outside the box.

If you don't understand, ask questions. It is not out of bounds to ask for help from a real live lawyer.

As a rule, though, the writer's goal is always to limit the publisher to only what that publisher needs and for only as long as that publisher needs it. As different technologies have progressed this is sometimes easier said than done. Most publishers of short stories will be asking for worldwide rights in the English language (or in whatever language they are publishing in). There can also be clauses or riders that will cover additional uses. For example, some publishers want the right to reprint a story in later collections, or the right to release the story in both print and audio formats. It's perfectly fine for the publisher to ask for these rights, but recalling that this is a negotiation, it is also perfectly fine for you to ask to be paid additional usage fees for these additional rights—or to have them struck completely.

WORD COUNT VS. FLAT RATES: The majority of publishers' submission guidelines outline their pay rates, and if you're actively working you probably already know them all. But if you are a writer fresh off the conveyor belt, I'll note here that some publications will pay flat rates for a short story, and some will pay a rate based on word count.

. . .

ROYALTY SPLIT PROJECTS: I'm including this here because over the past couple years it has become the practice of some small-press publishers to form a syndicate of writers who contribute work to a project in which they will be paid only by a split of royalties on actual sales. There are perfectly good reasons to decide to join these, and I have done that myself. But it is valuable to keep in mind that when you join these you are using up first publication rights.

RIGHTS REVERSION: A contract should not be open-ended, meaning it should always explain how long a publisher holds the right to print the story. Some ask for up to two years. Others are shorter. In addition, most contracts include a notice about how long after the story is published a publisher's exclusivity will last —in other words how long a writer is restricted from relicensing their intellectual property.

The first is important because without it the publisher is literally capable of keeping the work forever simply by not publishing it.

The second is important because reprinting a story—especially in today's fluid independent markets—can be lucrative.

PAYMENT ON ACCEPTANCE: Ah, sweet Nirvana. The best thing a writer of short stories can hear is that they will be paid on acceptance. Established publishers will tend to do this, but several cannot. Publishing houses that handle short fiction are not generally made of money, so they tend to run on skimpy budgets and if they pay on acceptance, they'll be keeping an inventory of unpublished work they've paid for that is sometimes a year or more deep—hence they've not received cash flow that covers that payment.

Payment on acceptance is good for the writer, of course,

because it protects us from potential demise of the publisher (which I'll dig into in a moment), and because of the time value of money—I would certainly rather have $400 now than $400 a year from now. Payment on acceptance places all financial risk on the publisher.

Payment on Publication: As a writer, I'd prefer to stay away from payment on publication, but unfortunately for writers the practice—while not ubiquitous—is at least somewhat standard. As a businessperson, I can understand it. As I noted above, payment on acceptance can be a substantial investment of capital for a publisher of short fiction. Something goes wrong for a few business quarters and they're dead.

So, it's hard for me to get so spun up about payment on publication that I don't license material this way. Depending on the market, and the IP, I'm fine with it.

A writer needs to understand what they are doing, though.

First, in practical terms this practice means cash flow may not happen for months or even years after acceptance. Agreeing to not be paid until publication is equivalent to giving the publisher a free option—meaning that you can't market the piece while publication is in process, and that the publisher isn't taking financial risk regarding your story by laying out cash up front. I'll talk about options more in a few moments, but for now let's concentrate on this contract. Payment on Publication means that if, by whatever nuances of fate, the publisher chooses not to publish your work (bankruptcy or simply changing their mind, for example), they are under no obligation to pay you for the time your IP was off the market.

Remembering that this is a negotiation, it can be worth asking that a Kill Fee be included in the agreement. Or simply that you are paid up front.

The worst that can happen is that the publisher says no.

. . .

<u>KILL FEES</u>: Kill fees suck. On occasion a publisher will accept a story, but then not be able to print it. This could happen for a few different reasons, the most frequent is that the company goes out of business, but I've also had cases in which the editor simply bought too many words and the book didn't have physical space available.

In cases where you've signed a contract that pays on acceptance, that Kill Fee is generally—but not always—simply the money already paid. In payment on publication agreements, that Kill Fee can be $0.

Bottom line is this: The most optimistic way of looking at a Kill Fee is that their existence proves that I'm not in this for the money—when I was new to the business, a Kill Fee felt like a stab in the heart, but even as a more established writer, they come with at least a spoonful of depression.

Welcome to the world of short fiction. Especially in the traditional markets.

<u>LIABILITY</u>: Every contract will include some clause in which the writer asserts their ownership of the rights being licensed and holding the publisher free of liability for damages brought if the manuscript is found to contain someone else's copyrighted material.

First—don't steal.

Let me reiterate. Do Not Steal.

Learn copyright law, and Don't Steal.

That said, I'd strongly suggest that writers read these sections and ensure that the wording limits liability to only cover publishers after such claims are proven in a court of law. Otherwise, a publisher may find it in their best interest to simply settle a claim out of court and pass the expense on to you.

. . .

<u>Options</u>: If you publish often enough, or just capture lightning in a bottle early, there is a reasonable chance someone will eventually approach you with a request to option your story for the purpose of making a film, or web show, or series, or video games, or various other derivative rights.

When this happens, you are allowed to give a little cheer.

It's a fun idea, right? The idea of seeing your work on a screen is mighty magnetic.

At its root, an option is an agreement in which the producer in question pays you to keep your IP off the market—i.e., not to sell those rights to anyone else (which is why I say payment on publication gives away a free option). As a rule, it will be a flat fee, and run for a set amount of time. As always, everything is negotiable.

Dealing with derivative rights, however, is a very complex world—far outside the scope of this little book—and unless you are a copyright lawyer, you'll not want to go it alone.

My suggestion is, after giving that little cheer, you respond with something that thanks the producer for their interest, then immediately reach out to established authors or entertainment IP lawyers to ask questions and get real advice.

Reviews

THERE ARE APPARENTLY two kinds of writers—those who read their own reviews and those who do not.

I am sorry to admit that I am one who will read a review of my own work, though I'm not sure I consider the practice as being particularly healthy. It's not, actually. But I'm too self-aware and too honest to be able to pretend I don't look at them.

The desire to know what someone thought about me is not something I'm particularly fond of (and my work *is* me, right?), but knowing reviews exist are like knowing there are brownies in the kitchen. They'll sit there and call me, and the more I resist the stronger the call…until I give up and go get the damned brownie.

But it's also like knowing there's going to be a car wreck outside my window. I can't not look.

Brownie or car wreck, I'm just going to *have* to check into it.

I am the one, after all, who as a kid created a homemade book and topped it with the New York Times blurb declaring "Collins Is Great!"

AMONG THOSE WRITERS who read their reviews, particularly among those who are publishing independently, there exists a subset who live by the creed that a writer can and should use reviews to adjust their work. They want to appeal to their fans by writing to the market, which is a sentiment that is—like trying to please your boss at work—I suppose at least grounded in a good place.

This is not why I read my own reviews, and in fact, these are not the reviews I'm talking about.

When independent writers use reviews to judge their market, they are routinely talking about customer reviews on Amazon. I suppose this makes some sense. I've been in Corporate America, after all. I understand satisfying the customer, and if that works for them, more power to it.

When it comes to short stories, though, I don't mean customer reviews—short stories in the independent world are probably not ever going to garner that much attention.

I'm talking about critics. The myriad of places that pay someone to judge fiction.

Two Thumbs Up.

I don't know exactly why I care about reviews. In fact, the truth is that I don't really care *what* the review says. I can't, for example, recall ever reading a review—positive or negative—and having it change anything about my work at all.

My advice is to ignore them if you can and forget them regardless of their assessment.

But I do care that they exist.

I have been known to scan the pages of *Locus* or *Tangent* or any of a few others to see if they've commented on anything I've done. A review is the circle of life, you see—the validation scene at the end of the story. A review means someone read my work. And that, simply for that moment in time, I existed as a piece of another person's life.

For just that moment, my work mattered.

Dealing with Rejection

Let's face it—people who reject our writing are mean and evil and should be launched into space from the world's biggest, wildest, and most whiplashiest catapult ever designed.

Yes, I bite my thumb at them.

I hope they get slivers from the wood as it whips them out to space.

That said, I want to talk about rejection.

Given the pure math of traditional publishing, most stories submitted to editors have to be rejected. There's only so much space—or money—available, so even if every story ever written was literally perfect, most would have to be passed on (thank God for indie publishing, right?).

Of course, every manuscript ever created is not…perfect.

In fact, none of them are—even the ones I like to consider so. None.

Beyond that, some stories won't hit the editor's vision, or they will hit an editor's anti-cookies, or…well, for those reasons and hundreds of others, they get rejected.

To work in the world of short fiction is to be able to withstand being told no early and often. When I was new and manuscripts were mailed, a rejection might come after three months or six months—now they can come in three to six hours. Talk about progress! I mean, sometimes that post-story afterglow hasn't even faded before your baby comes back all dinged up with its first scar.

So, odds are high that you're going to be dealing with rejection for a large part of your creative life—and rejection hurts. This means that so much of being a professional writer—especially in the traditional market—is going to be about developing your own personal reaction to rejection.

Some people brush it off.

I went through a phase where each rejection was a badge of honor, going so far as to keep a section of my website I called "The Accept-O-Matic" in which I publicly reported the huge number of rejections I received versus the pitifully small number of acceptances.

Yes, a certain dark sense of humor might be your cup of tea, too.

If there's good news here it's that rejection will generally not be so public. It will mostly come as an email in the privacy of your home, giving you a few moments to decompress before moving on. No one else needs to know your dreams have been squashed to bits just then, right? You don't have to tell anyone you've been rejected something over 1,200 times, like I have. You can if you want to, of course. Commiseration can be a great form of therapy. But you don't have to.

And when your significant other asks why ice cream is suddenly on the menu, you can either tell them of your rejection, or not—and assuming they love you as much as my wife loves me, they'll keep that question for another day.

Whatever your way of dealing with rejection, though, you should plan to get familiar with using it.

The most important thing is to build resilience.

Get knocked down. Get back up again.

I remind myself that a rejected manuscript is just a manuscript that hasn't found its audience.

It can feel like I'm lying to myself even when I know I'm not. But one of the surest ways I've found to fail is to focus on the idea that I *must* sell work immediately out of the box for it to be successful. It's an easy trap to fall into. It's a tough world, and sometimes I just want it to be less tough.

This is a complex psychology.

And it doesn't help that, while most rejections are quick and to the point, it can sometimes happen that an editor is not particularly kind. I once received a rejection with a handwritten note that read "this story barks," which I certainly laugh at now but at the time had me considering voodoo dolls and hairpins.

Editors are human, though.

They have their own personalities.

They can miss the point, and they come with their own wide background of baggage and expectation.

It happens.

I'm sure the "barks" guy wasn't trying to hurt anyone on purpose.

So, yes indeed, rejection is just hard, especially if the story is particularly dear to you—especially if that story matters.

IF YOU PAY ATTENTION, you also learn by watching other writers.

Perhaps that sounds a bit maudlin or even a hair sadistic, but if nothing else paying attention to other writers can make you feel better about these mini setbacks simply by letting you know you're not alone.

I had lunch once with another writer who asked how many times a story should be rejected before either trunking it or publishing it themselves. My answer was a bit rambling, but along the way I mentioned that I've been rejected well over a thousand times, and that I still get rejections. My personal record for most rejections on a story that eventually found a home is 44, and, in fact, that very day I had stories both rejected and accepted.

This surprised her.

Every working writer I know still gets rejected. This is a fact.

Stories get rejected for a lot of reasons, many of which are not related to quality.

A story that Trevor Quachri at *Analog* loves may well get the quickest of form rejections from John Joseph Adams at *Lightspeed*.

The process puts writers through an emotional wringer, but that is life.

Keep it on the market to find its proper place.

Creatives and Real Jobs

THE WORLD of creative people can feel intimidating. I mean, these people, they're so full of energy. And I'm just little old me.

You're going to have to just jump in, though.

Really you are.

Creative people are as different from other people as the work of creating art is different from the work of a "real" job. I've spent a lot of time in both environments, and while both have their moments, I can tell you which one best allows you to be the real you.

To explain, let me diverge first into the world of a "real" job.

A "REAL" JOB

I always felt like the best thing about having a "day job" with a company was working with other people to achieve things bigger than I could manage myself. This can be a lot of fun. To this day I take pride in things my work teams accomplished.

Ultimately, though, the fact that your work relies on others—both what you are charged with accomplishing and its quality—molds the experience in a myriad of ways, both good and bad.

Working in teams means you've got a bit of a safety net around you, and for the long run that can be comforting. To be blunt, it means you can be blazingly good for a while, then half-ass it at other times, and things will still work out. There's a momentum to a workplace, right? Other people are there to pick you up when you're feeling down. Sometimes you can surf the wake of those other great people and sometimes you drive the boat while carrying them.

Either way, you succeed or fail as a team.

There's a certain beauty to this situation, not the least of which is that being with a team of great people can help you ignore a lot of what are often otherwise quite caustic parts of the work environment.

Not every team, however, is so great. You might find George over there is more than the tiniest bit aggressive, or Fred is a closet asshole with tendencies toward sabotage, or … And even in the best of situations a corporate environment can suck your soul. The company always wants more, and there's a tax associated with getting too far out from the norm. Try as you might to fight through them there will always be certain sets of controls that exist in corporations that, assuming you look closely enough, you come to realize will never really work in your favor.

Corporate teams—especially the bad ones, but sometimes even good ones—can be riddled with in-fighting, backbiting, and other difficult interactions.

Poor team dynamics come in hundreds of forms, but I'm going to focus on one for a moment because it applies most directly to your life as a writer.

Opportunity.

There are only so many spots in an organization, and, at its root, the corporate game is organized as a tournament system. To advance I need to compete with my co-workers. And if *I* get a juicy role there's one less for them. The higher I go, the more rugged the competition gets—and that's before we even begin to open the lid on the jar of the numerous unintentional (or not ubintentional) biases inherent in how organizational power structures distribute these opportunities.

This dynamic exists in even the best of corporate environments. Succeeding and advancing in a company is about *both* performing and balancing these dog-eat-dog politics in a way that's deft enough to get ahead and strong enough to stay ahead.

When you work in a corporation, there's almost always someone around to help you learn the ropes, at least enough to help *them*, but there will also be folks who *do not* want to help you. You've worked with those people, right? People who see the idea of training you or giving you the spotlight means they risk their current or future job. Ever wonder why most mentoring in a company is done top-down? Think about it. At its heart, working a "real" job means working with people who often see that it's in their best interest if you don't … um … optimize your success.

I'll leave this conversation here, though, because the point I want to make is that even though writing for a living can feel competitive, especially for writers trying to break into traditional publishing, it has never been *completely* true. Or at least not true in the same way it is in the corporate environment. And in today's world where writers can go straight to the reader, it's not true at all.

Welcome to Write Club

YES, traditionally published magazines and anthologies have only so many words, and book publishers only so many slots. Yes, *getting into* the traditional publishing mill can very much feel like a tournament gig. And with traditional *book* publishers it doesn't stop there.

A big publishing house has only so many marketing dollars in their budget, only so many top slots, only so many book tours, only so many …

Some writers get a bunch. Others don't.

So, given that traditionally published writers are competing for limited resources in this way, it's easy to envision the idea of a writing career as the same zero-sum game built into corporate worlds. If you win, I lose, and vice versa. There is a truth there, and the fact that the relative value of our product is so much harder to define than the relative value of a corporate worker's output adds another even more horribly complex conversation to the writer's world.

Note the dangerous word *value* sitting up there like a silent landmine, eh?

But that view ignores the very real rules of Write Club.

What are the rules of Write Club?

Well, since you asked…

1. The First Rule of Write Club is that long-term success is *always* about building readership.
2. The Second Rule of Write Club is that any success *you* have in achieving the first rule does nothing to hurt the chances of *mine*.

3. The Third Rule of Write Club is that it's okay to talk about Write Club.

Don't believe me? Let's take a look.

RULE (1) <u>LONG-TERM success is always about building a readership.</u>

IN THE INDEPENDENT WORLD, this is obvious. Your eventual success, financial or otherwise, comes directly from your readership. Sure, you can and probably should, to some degree, package things to your advantage, or play pricing games, or do all sorts of other stuff that might improve your sell-throughs, but at the end of the day those things only go so far.

If people don't like reading your stuff, you're back to square one.

If they do, they'll follow you.

It's the same in the traditional world. A publisher can do things to manipulate opportunity, but that only forms the process. Readers still need to like your stuff well enough to say, "Hey, I wonder what else this writer's done?" When that happens often enough, you've got a financially successful career. Otherwise, you're back to square one.

That's a stressful thing in the traditional world because you have to play the tournament game just to get to the point where you have an opportunity to find a readership. In other words, as a new writer or even a not-so-new writer, you struggle to get past the editor, then you're subject to the corporate resource grab, and finally, when your work is published—and only when your work is published—you get to the point where you begin to find out if you might have a following.

How many writers on three-book contracts have been dumped when books one and two didn't garner them readership? To get that far, and then "fail," can be depressing.

** ASIDE: I was talking with a friend of mine some years back, a very good writer whose debut book had just been published. Book two was in the pipeline. I asked how things were going. "Okay," the writer replied with this oddly complex expression. "I'm just waiting for the numbers." A few months later this writer got a new contract. The numbers, in this case, were very, very good. That writer is a biggish name today, but at that time was in the limbo land of waiting to see if they had the beginnings of a readership.*

RULE (2) <u>Any success you have in achieving the first rule does nothing to hurt the chances of mine.</u>

LIKE THE FIRST RULE, the truth of this one exists everywhere but is most easily seen in the independent world.

I have many friends who sell lots of books through their independent publishing houses. None of their sales will ever affect one of mine—unless, of course, I get some extra readers due to good word of mouth between our readerships (there's that word *readership* again, eh?). In the independent model, a sale by another writer will never hurt me, and might even help.

This is a reason you'll often see independent authors working together.

The traditional model is, however, no different when it comes to the second rule of Write Club. To see this clearly, though, I have to once again ignore the fact that a writer is forced to play the tournament game just to get the opportunity to find a readership—which is shitty, but not relevant. Instead, I focus on what happens after they are accepted into the game. Once a writer is published it's easy to see that, when Stephen King sells a book, it doesn't change much of anything as to whether I will or will not sell a book.

If anything, if my name was Kings, way back in the old days of bookstores being the primary outlet, my Kings pseudonym would have sold more books simply due to proximity to Stephen King. At least that was the thought back then. Today it's more about Amazon's "Also Bought" list, which has a similar, though certainly different, dynamic.

That said, I know writers who would disagree with me on this idea that other writers are not my competition, writers who carry scars from the struggle against the tournament model of traditional publishing and are now bitter toward and even jealous of those who have been passed through the system to arrive at their opportunity. It is a truism to say the traditional publishing model is competitive. For those writers, the idea behind the second rule of Write Club is sometimes impossible to see, better yet accept. Yet, there it is.

Gathering readership, however, is not a tournament game.

** Aside: This is a reason I do not like the Kindle Unlimited subscription model and other exclusive subscription services of the ilk. They blow the Second Rule of Write Club out of the water. These systems pit writer against writer because Amazon or any other coordinator sets a defined market size, then tells writers to go compete for it. If my books are in KU (which today they are not), and I get a read, I get a slice of the pie and every other slice gets smaller. My sale hurts you, and vice versa. This is a huge change in the base dynamics of the market that I don't see a lot of writers talking about, and a reason I will refrain from using that market unless it literally becomes the only one available.*

THE SECOND RULE of Write Club is a big deal because it's something that completely separates the life of a career writer from the world of a corporate worker.

When writers understand and accept this second rule, it changes everything.

Which brings us to...

RULE (3) <u>It's okay to talk about Write Club.</u>

WHY DO writers (meaning mostly me!) go to workshops, conferences, and conventions? Why do we form writers' groups?

At a base level, it seems obvious, right? Writing can be a lonely business. It's nice to have human companionship. But it's more than that. A lot more.

Talking about Write Club is the very best way to learn about the business aspect of a writer's existence. Things are constantly changing. New tools are developed, and new platforms spring up like the proverbial Whack-A-Mole carnival game. The more chatter, the better you are able to see what things might work for you.

It's also another way to improve your craft. The best is simply to write more, but if you can find the right craft workshop at the right time, you can certainly amp your learning.

Part of the challenge of using Write Club well is to understand what it is you want to focus on. The primary purposes of conventions and workshops, for example, are quite different. Conventions are mostly geared toward self-promotion and business networking, while workshops are generally focused on a specific topic of craft, or business, or anything else. Both are great opportunities to join Write Club, specifically because—duh—this is where you find writers.

The world of Write Club is beautifully serendipitous at its core.

As long as I step into the environment, learning tends to find me exactly when I need it.

When *I* think of Write Club these days, I tend to think first about the network of Oregon writers and the Anthology workshop, which I attended quite often because it was so unique, and because writers kept coming *back* to it. But it applies to anything that works for you: Established craft programs like Clarion, Odyssey, Viable Paradise, or more business-oriented conferences like Superstars or the more recent 20BooksTo50K. It can apply to some local groups, too, depending.

The question is why attend them, right?

Especially the pricey events.

I can practice on my own for free, so why pay money to attend a workshop?

Wouldn't I be better off writing?

Well?

It's complex, especially for writers of short stories who—let's face it—are generally never going to make a real living unless they branch out. Quick math says that if I license ten stories of 6,000 words in a year for $0.08 a word, which is a fair professional rate for speculative fiction as I'm writing this, I can maybe make north of $4,800. That's … not a lot of money. Any reasonable person can see issues with that projection, too, not the least of which is that, especially early in a writer's career, one's chances of licensing ten short stories in a year are not high. By that I mean, it's not going to happen. And, even if it does happen, your word count could wind up lower, or your pay rate might dip a little.

Then we look at the expenses side of the ledger and see these workshops are not inexpensive.

Viable Paradise costs $1,100 as I write this. Clarion is $5,500 and six weeks of time. When it was running, the Anthology workshop cost some $700. Of these three, only Clarion's total included room and some food. For a short story writer, that investment represents a whale's portion of your income.

Yet still we go to conferences and workshops.

Why?

Well, welcome to Write Club.

Lessons I Have Learned from Write Club

A WRITER'S career evolves more than it develops.

When I first realized this, I did not like it. I am an engineer, you see. I like to think life progresses on a path that should be both linear and observable. I started my career at the origin point of 0, 0 on the graph, with time on the X-axis. As that time dimension progresses, my career should move forward in a smooth and obvious fashion.

Onward and upward!

That's how it was supposed to be.

You can laugh at me now.

As time has progressed, while I haven't come to exactly love it, I *have* come to see this evolutionary cycle for the wonderful thing it is.

This understanding is why I rarely go to writers' *conventions* anymore, but I still often attend *workshops*. Perhaps this will change as I evolve again, but the advantages I gained at a convention, things like contact with editors and the ability to pontificate on a panel or two, no longer tend to help me achieve the goals I'm currently interested in as a writer. I've come to understand that my manuscripts alone will speak for me when it comes to an editor's read, and that the readers I might gain from sitting on a panel are probably not any greater than I'd gain by simply writing more stories.

That's my view today, anyway.

In the stage I am at now, a convention is a tool for self-promotion, but I attend workshops to learn and acquire more skills. The primary value I look for in either is the opportunity to interact with other writers to better understand the shifting sands of the world around me. While I can do that at conventions, I note that, like me, other writers at conventions also seem to see them as self-promotional tools and thus are not always as focused on the things I care to focus on.

A workshop environment is much more conducive to this.

Regardless of the environment, I think it's fair to say that I have picked up a few bits and pieces over my time as a writer both of short stories and novels.

I thought it might be a good idea to put at least a few of them down here.

THE BEST WAY TO learn craft is always to practice it.

The second-best way to learn craft is to listen to other writers talk about it, or watch other writers do it (that is, devour and deconstruct other manuscripts). Reading about craft is fun, but I've rarely been able to translate other people's ideas about craft into anything that will actually help my own work.

THE EXCEPTION to this is story structure.

Story structure can be learned. Story structure can be taught. It is the "Math" of storytelling. For me, a great workshop taught by a great instructor worked wonders. After that, a writer is really on their own. This is because writing is personal, and there is only one me.

KEEP THINGS ON THE MARKET.

Corollary: This will get really hard after any piece has had three rejections, but do it anyway.

———

PUBLICATION IS MARVELOUS, but the writing itself is where the joy is.

———

A CAREER in writing (short stories or not) is about moving forward. I knew this intellectually from the beginning, but the emotional foundation of being a creative took a while to take. Write Club is amazing for this, though.

Once published, especially in a traditional market, a story can seem to fade quickly away. And that can feel oddly traumatic. I worked so hard on it, after all. And I loved it. I wanted people to admire it from all the same angles I admired it from while I was writing it.

Alas, it is not always so.

Short stories—especially—will have a short shelf life.

The beauty is to move on.

To always be writing.

I cherish every writer I see going through that, and I smile every time someone I care about publishes a new piece.

Me included.

———

THE BEST WAY TO become comfortable as a writer is to find communities of other writers.

———

IF YOU FIND the right communities of writers, you will learn things exactly when you need them.

This is true everywhere but is particularly true in the world of independent publishing.

It's a big, messy world out there, right?

I've learned things that I didn't even realize I needed to learn, merely because I arrived at a workshop in the right frame of mind to learn it and happened across someone who was at the right moment in their own journey to help me figure something out.

Things happen when they happen.

If you have questions, ask them. If you don't have questions or are afraid to ask them, then just listen to conversations going on around you. It will be hard to *not* come up with a bunch of questions by the time you're done. Things I've taken home include conversations about almost anything you can imagine when it comes to presenting my own work: Book design. Cover assessment. The best tools to package books with. Use of ISBN. The many ways people schedule their lives. How to deal with disappointment. Promotions. Easy marketing steps. Podcasting. The use of audio. The grind of the long tail. The big bump release. How short fiction sells and doesn't. How to leverage my short fiction in other ways. Series writing. Standalones. Amazon algorithms. Kobo promotions. The use of universal links. How to incrementally make things work. Hiring copy editors.

I mean…seriously, you name it, you'll hear it.

If you find the right community for you, the raw number of chance encounters with writers—who are all over the map when it comes to how they are becoming or have become professional writers—means that you are almost guaranteed to come away having learned whatever it was you needed to learn at that moment in time.

IF YOU HAVEN'T FOUND that community, it's okay to look harder. Write Club wants you.

WHEN THINGS GET TOUGH, simplify.

ONE OF THE biggest impediments that writers and particularly short story writers have with fitting into the world of independent publishing is that the process is too big.

I feel that, too.

You go to the internet to get advice and it's like you get slapped with a wave of 10,000 "Have to dos!" 10,000 things! I mean, geez. I'm lucky if I can remember to get dressed some mornings—don't tell me I have to do 10,000 things just to have a chance to be successful.

That advice will get all of my most delicate muscles to cramping up right quick.

This opportunity to see other writers—real people in various stages of getting their minds around what the publishing industry means to them—is valuable because it can change the feeling of being a writer from overwhelming to achievable.

That, no—you *don't* have to do *everything* to succeed. You just need to find a place to start that feels right for you, and then put one foot in front of the other. "Yeah," you'll hear someone say. "I think I'll try that." But you'll also hear "that's not for me" or "I'm not ready for that" or something else that will show you without doubt that there are very few "have to dos" in this world except for that first rule of Write Club.

Eventually a writer has to find a readership.

Focusing on one thing at a time is doable.

ONE CONVERSATION CAN CHANGE your life.

While I was still working a corporate job, I came upon a person who was maybe a year ahead of my situation—a guy who had just come from a lifetime of success in a corporate job but who had just become a fulltime writer. I walked away from that workshop with three important things to think about: (1) a confirmation that it was okay and even normal to be angsty about changing my life like that, (2) the image of this writer's smile as he talked about what life was like now, and (3) a firm idea of how to plan for the transition that I was likely to make.

It's not going too far to say that this single workshop helped changed my life.

YOU CAN DO a lot by focusing on 250 words a day.

CONTACTS IN WRITE Club come in all shapes and sizes.

Another workshop brought me into contact with the artist who later did a fantastic job on a set of kick-ass covers for my entire fantasy series. Without Write Club, I'd have never had those covers, and without them my work wouldn't sell as well.

A year later I reached out to several writers I had first met at a workshop to help me plan the launch of that same eight-novella fantasy series. To each I described the project and asked simply "what would you do?" Then I sat back and listened. Each one of those conversations added to my plan. I took lots of ideas that worked for me, and left the rest.

Every one of those books made the top ten of its categories on Amazon, and still sell today.

Of course, one of the reasons that series still sells today is that, at another workshop, one of the more experienced independent publishers in attendance looked at me and asked why I wasn't boxing them. "Tell me more," I replied.

An hour later I had an easy-to-follow strategy for how to bundle, price, and release three different box sets in such a way as the standalones would still be viable.

I can go on like this for several more pages.

I've gotten blurbs from Write Club members.

Ideas on covers.

Access to helpful resources.

Literally hundreds of lessons that I wouldn't have otherwise received.

Invitations to anthologies and other cool projects, both traditional and independent. My participation in Mercedes Lackey's Valdemar anthologies, for example, came through the magical synchronicity of fortuitous circumstances at a workshop.

You might find people to trade labor with. For example, trade cover design for copy editing services. Or book design, or whatever. You offer a strength, someone else will probably offer theirs. You never know what's going to happen.

I gave an interview to a writer who was doing a business book on project management—which, essentially, is my only real corporate skill. A year later, that writer brought me a copy of the book.

Very cool.

***

THERE'S MORE OF COURSE, but I think that gives you the idea of how Write Club works.

If you haven't experienced Write Club, just dive in. Someone will love you.

Collections

As you might expect, I love collections of short stories. To clarify terms, an anthology is a bunch of stories by a bunch of authors. A collection, however, is a bunch of stories by a *single* author.

As I write this, I have released three of them myself and have plans for at least four more. I also have a collaborative collection of racing-themed science fiction co-written with my friend John C. Bodin. So, yeah, I really do love collections of short fiction. If a short story does give us that dram of the writer's soul, a collection of short stories lets us into something bigger.

If a short story is a still photo, a collection is a slide show.

You settle into your seat, then in the dim lights and while the projector (he says, dating himself) gives its quiet little hum, you crack open the book.

Click-cha.

Story one, ooooo....

Click-cha.

Story two, ahhhh....

Click-cha.

A great collection builds on itself. Every story is different. The writer is the same, but as a reader I get to watch them pay with new ideas or new perspectives. For my taste, Karen Joy Fowler's *Black Glass* is like that. Lisa Silverthorne's *The Sound of Angels*, too. N.K. Jemisin's *How Long 'Til Black Future Month?* is another perfect example. These are three collections that I sometimes pick up and skim through just to let my eyes brush up against their table of contents. One of the stories will inevitably pull me down into the book, but I'm often surprised by which one.

It will be a different story every time.

Maybe that says something about me. Maybe the stories I select are barometers of my emotional state, stealing into my psyche to let these writers give me what I need at the time. Or maybe it's nothing but the probability waves of quantum physics collapsing inside my neurons, resulting in random happenstance.

That's a great mystery in life, after all.

Perhaps they are both true.

All I can say with any level of certainty is that when I think of these collections of short stories, I feel close to the world.

They make me happy.

Rereading

READING a great short story for the second time (or third, or fourth, or…) is for me like listening to a favorite song over and over again. By now it's cliché to note that a song can take you back to a place or a time. Sometimes even a snippet will do it, right? A particular sound of a snare drum at the opening, or the unique tone of an organ coming in.

I'm the same way with short stories.

I have a handful of them I go back to on a periodic basis simply because I recall how they made me feel, and I want to feel that again. Harlan Ellison's work can do that to me. I love the energy of his words crashing together. Ray Bradbury has been on my list for the longest time. I love how his work makes my heart open. Karen Joy Fowler's "The Brew" is amazing from beginning to end but is one I go to for its simply perfect opening above all things. Then there's Lisa Silverthorne's collection *The Sound of Angels* that I love for its raw power and the staccato one-two punches inside its ordering of titles.

I update my "go to" list occasionally. My latest addition was "Coming Home," written by Chrissy Wissler. I'll admit that most of Harlan Ellison's work has fallen off my list, mostly because every time I read his work, it screws up my writing since I wind up trying to sound like him. But that's how it goes, right?

A reader evolves, too.

Sometimes this element of my love for short stories can get tangled up in music, too.

A long time ago, for example, when *The Magazine of Fantasy and Science Fiction* first published Jack Cady's breathtaking novella "The Night We Buried Road Dog," it happened that my copy of Neil Young's *Harvest Moon* album was on the CD player (remember those?), and that album became the soundtrack to the story. To this day, I can't hear "From Hank to Hendrix" without getting an intense surge of Cady's story. Similarly, when I think about the story, I invariably hear Neil Young.

Two for the price of one, baby!

That is how I roll.

REREADING MYSELF

Once they are published, I don't reread my novels. I know what happened, after all. And I know what I was thinking as I wrote them, so if I think about them just right, I can flash on how they felt. For me that's enough.

I'll sometimes page through one to pick out something at random, but the only time I really read them again are for continuity purposes. If I'm writing more in that world, I want to be consistent.

Short stories are different, though.

I'll sometimes pick up one of my stories and read through it, and when I do, I often find myself getting drawn into it again. There's something different about that experience. I think it has to do with the idea that I often write short stories to help me determine how I think about something—and that going back into these pieces brings a lot of that together again.

Is it still valid? Have I changed?

How embarrassing was that?

These are feelings like flipping through old photo albums.

The stories feel like my family.

Or like high school friends. Or college friends.

Like a snippet of my life—a brief encounter with a musician in an airport, or a chance encounter with two older women vacationing from Germany, or…

They are all parts of me, and I love them for that.

Coda

A COUPLE DAYS AGO, while I was in the process of completing this manuscript, I wrote a short story for a side project I'm involved in. Took about four hours and came out just as I'd wanted it to.

That happens sometimes.

I realize that in the pages of this book, I've spent considerable time dwelling on the travails and hardships of a creative life, but I'll say this, too. If I focus on the idea that being creative is supposed to be fun, if I can let myself Dare to Be Bad, if I can let myself simply write…well…eventually it has all worked out. And sometimes—most of the time, really—when I give myself to the page and let things go as they need to go, the Powers That Be reward me with this kind of story.

While writing this manuscript, I picked up my dog-eared copy of Lisa Silverthorne's collection that I mentioned previously, *The Sound of Angels,* and read three stories.

Sublime.

So, yeah, a life spent engulfed in short stories is a pretty good gig.

I highly recommend it.

Thank you so much for being part of it.

You've come to the end of *On Creating (And Celebrating!) Characters.*
If you enjoyed this book, you might like Ron's other explorations
of the writing life:

You might also consider leaving a review at your favorite online
bookseller. Even a few sentences can help!

Follow Ron!

Get updates on Ron's latest publications, and maybe even a few free books by joining!

Ron's Newsletter
http://typosphere.com/newsletter

Ron's Patreon
patreon.com/RonCollinsWrites

About Ron Collins

Ron Collins is a best-selling Science Fiction and Dark Fantasy author who writes across the spectrum of speculative fiction. With his daughter, Brigid, he edited the anthology *Face the Strange*.

His short fiction has received a Writers of the Future prize. His short story "The White Game" was nominated for the Short Mystery Fiction Society's Derringer Award.

He holds a degree in Mechanical Engineering and has worked to develop avionics systems, electronics, and information technology before chucking it all to write full-time.

Other Work by Ron Collins

<u>Novels</u>

Stealing the Sun (9 books)

Saga of the God-Touched Mage (8 books)

The PEBA Diaries (2 books)

The Knight Deception

Wakers

Fastballs and Fairies (3 Books), with Brigid Collins

Cruise Brothers Series (3 Books) with Jeff Collins

<u>Collections</u>

Collins Creek (3 volumes)

Tomorrow in All the Worlds

Picasso's Cat & Other Stories

Five Magics

Seven Days In May, with John C. Bodin

<u>Poetry</u>

Five Seven Five

<u>Nonfiction</u>

On Creating (And Celebrating!) Characters

On Being (And Becoming Again!) A Writer